J. Jemmett Browne

Lone Lassie

An Autobiography: Vol. II.

J. Jemmett Browne

Lone Lassie
An Autobiography: Vol. II.

ISBN/EAN: 9783337117726

Printed in Europe, USA, Canada, Australia, Japan

Cover: Foto ©Raphael Reischuk / pixelio.de

More available books at **www.hansebooks.com**

A LONE LASSIE

AN AUTOBIOGRAPHY

BY

J. JEMMETT-BROWNE

IN THREE VOLUMES.
VOL. II.

LONDON:

SAMPSON LOW, MARSTON, SEARLE & RIVINGTON,

CROWN BUILDINGS, 188, FLEET STREET.

1886.

CONTENTS OF VOL. II.

A LONE LASSIE.

CHAPTER I.

A PUZZLED BRAIN.

THOSE were happy days of mutual confidence and love. I could not let my new-found mother out of my sight. I followed her about, watching to anticipate every want before she could express it. I was up betimes that I might call her, bring her warm water, brush out her beautiful black hair. I was proud to be her waiting-maid.

I told her, by degrees, all the events of my life—my hopes, my fears, my joys, my sorrows. I was able to tell her of much kindness that I had met with—Nannie's devotion, the respectful love of Hamish Macpherson and his son and daughter, Kenneth and Elsie, the motherly care of Sister Lucy, Mrs. Annesley's affection.

I told her of my strange meeting with my father at Glen Shiel, and how he had spurned me like a loathsome thing. The tears ran down my mother's cheek, as she pressed me to her heart; but she said not a word in explanation of such cruel treatment. I told her of my unkind reception by my grandmother, and the indignities I met with in my father's house. Her eyes flashed as only Southern eyes can flash. She muttered something in Italian which I did not understand, and then added in English, "That woman is a demon; there is not a wickeder in hell."

Her anger subsided when I told her how lovingly Mrs. Annesley had mothered me, how Bertie had been more to me than a

brother. " God bless her, and him," she
prayed, with uplifted eyes, " and all who
have been kind to my poor child."

My mother encouraged me to speak of
Bertie Annesley, and I was not slow to
sing his praises. I told her how he had
been my constant companion till he went
to school, not despising me for my ignorance and weakness, but trying to make me
clever and strong as himself. I attempted
to describe his beautiful face, like that of
some Greek god, full of love and strength.
I told her of our adventure with the red
deer, and the joy I felt in the Verderers'
Hall when I heard Bertie's voice claiming
the poacher's punishment to save me and
the gipsies. It was pleasant to feel my
mother's arm tighten round me in approbation of our conduct. I could not help
growing eloquent when I talked of Bertie,
and my cheeks tingled with hot blushes
when I met my mother's sympathetic
glance. I had always thought that my

love for Bertie was only a sister's love for
a kind brother, and almost fancy that it
was the searching look in my mother's
eyes that led me first to know my own
heart; at all events, it was soon after I had
found a mother's love that I first acknowledged to myself that my love for Bertie
was deeper and more absorbing still. The
feeling grew with my happiness, and I
caught myself unconsciously blushing as
I looked at Mrs. Annesley, and wondered
if she guessed that my heart was filled
with the image of her son. I began to
feel that I had not sufficiently cultivated
her love, and this led me to try and make
up for past neglect. She sometimes looked
surprised as I did her little services; and
one day, after I placed a footstool for her
use, she thanked me sweetly, and begged
me not to think she was jealous of my
mother. "I am quite contented to be
second in your love," she added. She did
not guess that she was only third. Dear

Mrs. Annesley! I had long learned that a cold exterior can cover a warm heart.

My mother had been with us three days, and in that short time she and Mrs. Annesley had become fast friends. One seemed to complement the other. Mrs. Annesley was plain, honest, and practical; my mother, beautiful, talented, and perhaps a little too much given to the ideal. Both had loving natures, though they showed it in very different ways; and both had drunk deeply of the cup of sorrow. I saw that they had mutual confidences, for more than once they had stopped dead short in their conversation when I entered the room. I was rather inclined to be jealous, as my mother refused to relate to me the story of her unhappy life. She told me that I must exercise my faith, and take her word that there was no reason why I should not give her my whole heart. She had suffered terribly, had been cruelly treated, everything was against her, but my love was lightening the load she had to bear, and giving her strength to keep up a brave heart.

She bade me entertain no bitter feelings against my father. He did not know the truth. She was content that he should hate her—he had cause enough; but she loved him with all the love in her heart, and wished me to do the same. She even partially exonerated his mother, so far at least that she allowed there were circumstances unexplained which partially justified her conduct; but she told me that from the day she had come home as a bride, Lady Dampier had persecuted her, and adopted the vilest measures to rob her of her husband's love.

" Trust me," she added—" trust me till you are of age. If things remain as they now are, you shall then be taken into my entire confidence. You are too young and pure to understand half of what I should have to tell you. You will be a woman at one and twenty, and then in self-defence you must learn something of the ways of this wicked world; at all events, you will be better able to judge whether your unfortunate mother has been more sinned against than sinning."

"Trust you!" I cried; "I will trust you now and always. I will not listen to any explanation. If all the world slandered you, I would believe you to be good and pure and noble. You are my own dear mother. I love you as you love me, trust you as you trust me. There can be no doubts in perfect love."

I did not keep my promise long!

Next morning I was arranging flowers in our little dining-room. The house was so small that we seldom closed the doors into the tiny hall. I heard my mother and Mrs. Annesley in conversation. I was not listening, indeed I was humming over a Neapolitan barcarolle just above my breath. As the last words, " Vieni al mar," fell from my lips, I heard their voices more distinctly.

"Sorry as I shall be to lose you," said Mrs. Annesley, "I do not feel that I can honourably keep you as my guest. The Dowager has placed Nellie in my care, and pays for her board, lodging, and education. You are the last person she would wish to see in the child's company. It goes to my heart to say it, but you must leave us."

"I know you are right, Mrs. Annesley. I cannot expect you to betray your trust. I must go, though it seems very hard to leave my darling just as I have found her."

I felt choking, and was about to rush into the sitting-room and implore my mother not to desert me again. I waited, however, to recover my breath.

"Very, very hard," repeated Mrs. Annesley. "It does seem very cruel to separate mother and daughter, but I must not allow duty to wait on inclination. You see my position, dear Lady Dampier."

"You must not call me Lady Dampier," my mother answered, with a sob in her throat. "You know I have no right to the name. I am not Sir Lionel's wife——"

I dared not listen to another word. I had heard enough to overwhelm me with shame and sorrow. I crept out of the room, and out of the house through the back door. I ran through the orchard into the forest. I threw myself on the ground under a great beech tree, where the sunshine shimmered through the shivering leaves. But no sunshine fell upon my heart. All the world to me was cold and dark, and full of bitter grief and doubt. My mother was going to leave me! "I am not Sir Lionel's wife" kept on booming in my ears like the funeral knell of all my hopes and happiness. "I am not Sir Lionel's wife;" and I hid my face amongst last summer's dry dead leaves, dead as my poor heart.

I had always understood that I was the child of Sir Lionel and Lady Dampier. If my mother was not Lady Dampier, I could not be her daughter. If, on the other hand, I was her child, how could Sir Lionel be my father? Whichever way I looked, I was met by a paradox. I felt in a waking nightmare.

I did not wish to give up my birthright. I loved my father (if he was my father) with a strong filial love, which no unkindness on his part could destroy. His handsome face often smiled on me in my dreams, as it smiled on me that day on the mountainside, before the smile became a scowl. I loved my mother with a passionate love, and knew that my love was returned. If I had to give up one or the other, I would have given up my father, especially as it seemed that I could not be his child, if my mother was not his wife. My poor brain went round in trying to read the riddle. If I had only listened a minute longer, I might have heard something more definite and less puzzling, and I began to regret that I had not for once played the eavesdropper.

It never occurred to me, however, that any reflection on my mother's character could be deduced from her words. I was a simple country maiden, pure and guileless, totally unsophisticated. I had not tasted of the fruit of the tree of knowledge, of good and evil. I believed in my mother's goodness as I believed in a good God; but it was impossible to hear that she was not the wife of the man she professed to love so dearly, and encouraged me to love, without some inexplicable doubts taking possession of my brain. Something evidently was wrong in our family connection. It was a wearisome puzzle, a riddle without an answer.

I lay on the hard ground, looking up through the branches at the summer sky, as if I hoped to read the solution of the mystery in its blue depths, or on the fleecy clouds that sailed across them. But I could evolve no explanation, internally or externally.

I could not let the matter rest. I did not think it would be fair to question Mrs. Annesley; besides, I knew she was a woman who would never break a confidence. She was staunch and true to her friends, and there could be no doubt that she was now bound to my mother by ties of mutual confidence and friendship. I felt positive that my grandmother had imparted to her some facts to account for my deserted position, which had probably led her to discuss family matters with my mother. I should get no help from Mrs. Annesley. At first I thought of telling Bertie what I had overheard, but I felt a maidenly shrinking, unsophisticated as I was, from touching on the subject of matrimonial complications with a man; and Bertie was a man now, with a long yellow moustache.

I made up my mind to adopt the most straightforward course—to go direct to my mother and ask her to explain the strange words I had heard. I jumped up and ran in the direction of the cottage, burning to carry out my resolution.

Just as I came within sight of the ford, I heard the sound of carriage-wheels, a very unwonted sound in the recesses of the forest. The carriage must be near, for distant wheels could not be heard on a turfen road. I stood still to listen, and in a minute a carriage appeared, a carriage hired from the Crown Hotel at Lyndhurst. I recognized the driver. It crossed the ford and drew up at our garden-gate. A lady got out. She walked like an old woman, with the help of a stick. She entered the cottage. Full of curiosity, I crossed the footbridge, and ran up the slope to the back entrance. Mrs. Nutburn told me that an old lady was in the sitting-room. She had asked for Mrs. Annesley, and on hear-

ing that she was out, said she would
wait her return.

I went up to my room, smoothed my
hair, and shook off some moss and withered
leaves clinging to my frock. I ran downstairs, and opened the sitting-room door
timidly. The old lady was seated at the
table, turning over the leaves of a photo-
graph album. Her back was towards me.
She looked round, expecting to see Mrs.
Annesley.

I stood in the presence of my grandmother!

CHAPTER II.

"I AM expecting Mrs. Annesley every minute," I said, with as much politeness as I could muster, when addressing a woman who had treated my mother so shamefully and myself so unkindly. "She has only gone out for a short stroll in the forest. May I offer you some tea, or a glass of wine, after your drive?"

"No, thank you; I will wait your mother's return."

"Mrs. Annesley is not my mother."

"I thought you were too pretty a girl to be her daughter. By-the-by, I remember now she only had a son. May I ask who you are?"

" Your granddaughter, Nellie Dampier."

" You don't mean to say you have grown into a woman already! How long is it since I saw you in Eaton Square ? "

" More than five years, grandmamma," purposely laying stress on the grandmamma. I hoped to irritate the old lady into some explanation of the mystery uppermost in my mind.

" Don't grandmamma me ! " she cried, striking her stick emphatically on the carpet. " I told you not to do so in London. I repeat my order in the New Forest."

" You are my father's mother, so I must be your grandchild."

" You are not. I won't acknowledge you."

" But, grandmamma—— "

" Are you trying to put me out ? Take care, Miss Pert ! " And she shook her stick in my face.

"I wish you would tell me who I am, Dowager Lady Dampier."

"Don't call me 'Dowager.' I am not the Dowager, I am plain Lady Dampier."

"Well, then, plain Lady Dampier——"

"I won't be treated with this disrespect by a chit like you!"

"What am I to call you? You are not my father's mother, you are not the Dowager, you are not plain—I will call you pretty Lady Dampier. Will that do?" I asked, with complete gravity.

"Are you a knave or a fool?"

"I should prefer being a fool to a knave," I said, emphasizing the last word, and looking her full in the face.

"Do you mean to insinuate that I am a knave?" Lady Dampier asked, blazing into a passion, and striking me a blow on my arm.

"You are a cruel, wicked old woman!" I cried, in much pain. "I hate you! I am very glad I am not your grandchild.

I should be ashamed at having such a grandmother!"

Lady Dampier got up from her chair. She was trembling with passion. I do not know what she intended to do or say.

The door opened, and my mother walked into the room.

The two women stared at each other in mute astonishment. Anger and hatred blazed in the eyes of both. The old lady sank into a chair. My mother looked supremely grand and beautiful as she drew herself up to her full height, and withered my grandmother with the glance of a Medea.

" How dare you come into my presence?" shrieked the Dowager.

" I should certainly not have entered the room of my own will, had I known that Lady Dampier was in it," my mother answered, with assumed calmness.

" Be off, then, at once! Take yourself out of my sight, vile woman, or, by God, I shall strike you!"

"The God, whose name you take in vain will, one day, judge between us which of the two is vilest."

"Do you mean to say that I am what you are—a low, play-acting strumpet?" cried the old lady, trying to strike my mother in her impotent rage. Her gold-headed cane flew out of her hands, and broke the looking-glass over the chimney-piece. She seemed frightened for a moment at what she had done.

"Leave the room, Nellie; leave me with this foul-mouthed woman. I wonder even you, madam, can use such language before your granddaughter—a pure, spotless child."

"As pure and spotless as her mother!"—with a hideous laugh. "Give me my cane!" she continued.

"You might hurt my mother as you have hurt me;" and I threw the stick out of the window.

"Did your grandmother strike you?" asked my mother.

I showed her my arm, with a red
bruise.

"How dare you strike my child?" asked
my mother, towering over the old woman
like an avenging goddess, and then re-
straining her righteous anger as she looked
at me.—"Go, Nelly; go."

"I will not leave you alone with this
mad old woman, mother."

"Mad, am I?" shrieked the Dowager.
"I have had enough to make me mad,
when that shameless woman came between
me and my son, with her siren voice and
her wicked heart. You talk of your child
as if she was an angel of purity. Do
devils breed angels, Beatrice Ponsonby?
Take your devil's spawn, and get out of
my sight."

"May God forgive you! For Lionel's
sake, I will try and command myself."

"For Lionel's sake! I won't suffer his
name to be fouled by such lips as yours.
Much you cared for him! You, who

blasted his life, drove him from his home, sent him off a wanderer on the earth— wifeless, childless."

"Not childless, Lady Dampier," said my mother, with a voice full of tears.

"Yes, childless! Do you think we are idiots enough to accept your word for that girl's paternity? You, who deceived us, disgraced us in the sight of the world, dragged our name in the mire, broke a proud man's heart."

"Be merciful, if you hope for mercy," sobbed my mother, sinking on a chair, and burying her face in her hands. "If you knew all, you would not be so pitiless. God only knows how I have always loved your son, how I love him now! With appearances against me, I cannot expect you to believe my word."

"More than appearances," cried Lady Dampier, with a shrill laugh. "You were divorced in open court; you were proclaimed before all the world to be—— "

"Stop, Lady Dampier! Not before my child;" and she beckoned me to go."

"All the world knows you to be an adulteress!" shrieked the old lady so loudly that I could not help hearing it upon the stairs. There was a dead silence and a heavy fall. I ran back into the room. My mother was lying on the floor. Mrs. Annesley fortunately came in from her walk at this moment. With her calm, self-possession she took the case into her hands at once. She loosened my mother's collar, and, taking some flowers out of a basin on the table, sprinkled her face with water.

My mother opened her eyes, and took a long breath.

"Adulteress!" she muttered. "Oh! to think that I should ever be called by such a name before my child!"

"What has happened, Nellie?" asked Mrs. Annesley.

"I call the woman by her right name,"

said the Dowager, tottering on to her feet. "But spades don't like to be called spades."

"Lady Dampier!" cried Mrs. Annesley, whose attention had been so arrested by my mother's position on the floor that she had not noticed the old lady. "This is indeed a surprise."

"An unlucky surprise, you should say. I am passing through Lyndhurst, and did not like to be so near an old acquaintance without paying her my respects"—sarcastically. "I should not, however, have intruded had I known the kind of company you keep. After all the kindness I have shown you, I did not expect to find my son's divorced wife under your roof."

"I only discovered yesterday that my dear friend, Signora Bardi, had been Sir Lionel's wife. I had not the slightest suspicion, when I asked her to spend a few days with me, that such was the case. Nor had she the faintest idea that Nellie was her daughter."

"You expect me to believe such a ridiculous tale?" exclaimed the old lady.

"I am not in the habit of saying what is not true, Lady Dampier. It may seem a strange coincidence. I repeat, I only discovered yesterday who the signora really was, and this morning I told her, with great regret, but very distinctly, that it would be a breach of confidence if I allowed her to remain under the same roof with her daughter."

"I fully intended to have left to-morrow," said my dear mother, who had now recovered from her swoon.

"I might believe Mrs. Annesley's word," said the Dowager, "but not yours. Your whole life has been a lie."

"Once more I say, for Lionel's sake, I will command myself. May God forgive his mother. I will try and walk to my room. Nellie will come with me. You will not desert me, darling?"

"Never, mother; never."

"Take her, by all means!" shrieked the old lady. "I'll have nothing more to say to the baggage. Take her, and welcome. Like suits like—who knows, you may find a father to own her?"—with a hideous laugh.

"Perhaps I may," replied my mother, quietly; and she kissed me tenderly as we left the room together. "God grant I may, some day!"

CHAPTER III.

"ENTREAT ME NOT TO LEAVE THEE."

ONCE in her room, my mother fell on her knees by her bedside. Her whole frame shook convulsively, till a fit of sobbing seemed in some measure to calm her emotion. I knelt by her side, and, throwing an arm round her, implored her not to weep."

" Dry your eyes, dear mother," I whispered. " Do not let that wicked, mad, old hag have the satisfaction of causing you a single tear."

" Oh, my child ! to think that you should have heard such things said of me, heard me called by such foul names ! "

"Do not let that trouble you, mother. I did not understand what the woman said. If I did, it would not weigh a straw with me. I hate her, for my own sake as well as yours! She is a low-minded, vulgar creature, though she has a title. I don't believe she was born a lady; if she was, I am quite sure she won't die a lady."

"Lady Dampier was a clergyman's daughter."

"The nearer the church, the nearer the devil," I remarked, hoping by face-tiousness to check my mother's tears.

"I do believe the woman is a demon; she played the devil's part with me. You say, my child, you did not understand her shameful insinuations?"

"How should I, mother? I never heard such language before."

"You trust me still, Nellie, and do not believe that I am an abandoned woman?"

"I believe you to be as good as she is bad. I know there is some mystery about you and my father, but I won't and don't believe a word against my own dear mother. If either of you are in fault, I am sure it is not you."

" Your father is perfectly free from blame. I have ruined his life. His mother spoke truly there."

" You are trying to make me doubt you, mother. Tell me one thing, is Sir Lionel Dampier my father."

" Of course he is ! What can make you ask such a silly question ? "

" And you are my mother ? Then, you must be his wife."

" I must answer you truthfully. I am not your father's wife."

" Oh, mother, how can that be ? I have puzzled my brain over it till it is quite stupid."

" Then, some one has been trying to set you against me."

" No one. I should like to see any one dare ! "

"And yet you had heard that I was not your father's wife."

"I heard you say so yourself, mother. I was in the dining-room this morning, when you were talking to Mrs. Annesley. I heard you say, 'Don't call me Lady Dampier. I am not Sir Lionel's wife.'"

"Did you hear what followed?"

"No. I ran away. I had heard more than I wanted, and yet when I was fretting about it in the forest, I wished I had stayed and listened. I might have heard some explanation to satisfy my curiosity and dispel my doubts."

"You did doubt me, Nellie?"

"Not exactly, mother; but I thought something must be wrong if you were not really Lady Dampier. I had made up my mind to come and tell you what I had overheard, and implore you to take me into your confidence. I could not have slept a wink with such a puzzle in my brain."

"I told you the other day, dear child,

that there were passages in my life which I would reveal to you when you were of age. I thought you were too young and innocent to understand what I should have to tell you. I think so still; but what I could have kept to myself, before you heard me say that I was not your father's wife, and before his mother's gross language, I can no longer hide from you. I shall now tell you the whole mystery of my life."

"Not all, mother; keep the most of it till I am twenty-one, only tell me how you are not Lady Dampier."

"To answer that question involves everything; so I must make a clean breast of it, darling, and leave you to pass judgment on the whole of my conduct."

"I should never presume to judge any one, least of all my mother. But I need not hear the case to give my verdict. 'Not guilty' is written on your sweet, honest face."

"My conscience is quite clear of any

intentional sin, but still I cannot acquit myself of much blame."

"I should like to ask you one question,
mother. Were not you married to my
father, Sir Lionel Dampier?"

"I was married to him, not only in one
church, but in two. I was married with
the full rites of the churches of Rome and
England. I do not think I ever told you
that I am a Catholic."

"Protestant or Roman Catholic, you
must be Lady Dampier; you must be my
father's wife."

"May I come in?" asked Mrs. Annesley,
after knocking at the door.

We were still on our knees. We both
rose together, and I opened the door.

"You will be pleased to hear that old
Lady Dampier has left," said Mrs. Annesley. "She has made you suffer keenly,
signora."

"And me, too," I put in. "Look at the
bruise on my arm."

"She struck you, Nellie?" asked Mrs. Annesley. "What for?"

"Because I told her what I thought of her."

"You ought to have remembered she was your grandmother, Nellie," said Mrs. Annesley.

"That is just what she said she was not. Grandmother or no grandmother, she is a fiend."

"She is a bad, revengeful woman," said Mrs. Annesley. "Half-mad, I should think, from her behaviour downstairs."

"Not half-mad," I remarked; "quite mad. A dangerous lunatic by the way she handles her cane."

"How did you get rid of her?" asked my mother.

"She gave me the choice of turning you and Nellie out of the house this evening or losing her patronage."

"And you gave us the preference, dear Mrs. Annesley," exclaimed my mother. "How can we show our gratitude?"

"By making this your home as long as it suits your convenience. I am now free to choose my guests."

"You darling old mammie," I cried as I kissed Mrs. Annesley with juvenile impetuosity.

"I cannot be the cause of separating you from a kind and influential friend. Write to Lady Dampier and tell her that I am leaving you at once, and that Nellie is going with me."

"I shall do nothing of the sort. Do you think that I am going to part with my daughter, Nellie, in that abrupt fashion, or you either, dear friend?"

"I ruin all who love me," sighed my mother.

"And bring them a blessing at the same time," I cried. "It was a strange coincidence that brought you and grandmamma together. I wonder what she is doing in these parts. No good, I am sure."

"She told me," said Mrs. Annesley,

that she is on her way to some friends on the other side of the forest, and—— "

" Thought she might as well insult us *en passant*," interrupted I. " Well, I call it a happy coincidence, if it frees me for ever from her control."

" You will not hurry away now, signora?" said Mrs. Annesley. " We shall want some long talks about Nellie, and we have plenty of time for them. You are very worn out, and I am going to insist on your taking a rest. You will go to bed like a good little girl, and Nellie shall bring you up some supper."

My mother threw herself on Mrs. Annesley's neck, and sobbed her grateful thanks, whilst I covered her hands with kisses. How I wished Bertie could have seen the loving group, of which his mother formed the central figure! He would have been more proud of her than ever !

" I will indeed accept the invitation most joyfully," said my mother. " You have

taken one burden off a heavy heart. I shall
be able to look about me, and decide what
is the best for both of us. Lady Dampier,
in washing her hands of Nellie, means to
intimate that she will stop the supplies. I
will gladly undertake to make up for what
she takes away. But I expect Nellie will
like to follow my fortunes. We are all the
world to one another now, darling."

"Entreat me not to leave thee, not to
return from following after thee," I sang
to Gounod's beautiful setting of those touching words, "'For whither thou goest, I will
go . . . thy people shall be my people,
and thy God my God;' which means,
without music, that I will go to Italy with
you."

"And leave poor mammie?" cried Mrs.
Annesley, sorrowfully.

"Only for a time. Depend upon it, I shall
come back. I love the New Forest too
well to be long away from its oaks and
beeches;" and I blushed as I thought that

Bertie might some day come after me, and bring me back as his wife.

"You will be satisfied," said my mother, sadly, "to live with a mother who has lost her good name."

"Your name will always be good in my ears.—Mrs. Annesley knows your story, doesn't she, mother?"

"The whole, Nellie."

"You do not appear to have fallen in her estimation; why should you in mine?"

"You may well ask why, Nellie," exclaimed Mrs. Annesley. "I am proud to have such a noble woman under my roof;" and she patted my mother's hand in a loving manner, rather foreign to her reserved character.

I knew Mrs. Annesley to be a just woman, in no way influenced by sentiment. I looked upon her judgment as impartial and final. All my doubts were gone, if they had ever really existed. I was no longer eager to hear my mother's story.

"Do you know, kind friend," asked my mother, "that two little ears heard me repeat to you this morning that I was not Lady Dampier, not Sir Lionel's wife; and a little brain has almost become addled in attempting to solve the riddle?"

"And you have given her the key?"

"Not yet. I am going to tell her all —all that a girl can understand."

"I think you are quite right. Confidence begets confidence; but I am not going to allow you to excite yourself any more till you have slept off the effects of the painful scene you have gone through. Nellie is not so impatient that she cannot wait a few hours. She will be sadder for hearing the story of your blighted life."

"And happier, too," said I; "for I shall be able to give her my loving sympathy."

My mother insisted on my leaving her. She would try and sleep whilst I went down to supper. She could eat nothing herself. Rest was better than food after such an attack.

She was sleeping when I crept back into her room an hour later. She had loosened the long plaits of her wavy hair, which trailed over the pillow in rich dark masses. Her face was colourless, like that of some beautiful statue carved out of pure Carrara marble. In her white dressing-gown she looked so death-like that I shuddered till I saw the gentle heaving of her bosom. I sat down by her side, and took her hand gently in mine.

"Poor dear mother of mine!" I said to myself. "You were made to be loved. My father must have loved you once! What could have made him give you hate for love? He must return to you some day, when that wicked woman is dead. In the meantime, a daughter's love shall make up to you a little for the loss of a husband's."

She slept on long and soundly, worn out with the emotion which had affected

her so violently. The westering sun began to peep in. It threw upon the bed
shadows of the creeper sprays that festooned
the little window, and painted my mother's
pale cheek with the blush of evening.

At last her eyes opened, and, seeing me
beside her, she smiled a recognition, half
love, half sorrow.

" Have I been long asleep ? "

" It is eight o'clock."

" What a long siesta I have had! I
feel so much better in mind and body.
Nothing now can separate you and me.
It seems to open a new life of happiness.
I can almost thank your grandmother for
her insults."

" Don't call her my grandmother. I
repudiate the connection as she does.
Let us both forget that the earth is disgraced by the existence of such a reptile."

" Your language may be appropriate,
my child, but is over-strong. You have
not half so much to forgive as I have,

though I allow that there are extenuating circumstances in her favour. Perhaps you may exonerate her entirely, when you have heard my story. I am ready to begin it now."

"Wait till you are well again, mother. I am in no hurry for your revelations. They will keep a day, a week, a month, a year, or for ever. I wish you would let me fetch you something. You must be hungry."

"I think I could drink some tea, and then I should be equal to the effort."

"There," she said, handing me the empty cup, "I feel quite strong again. Come, Nellie, and lie down by my side. I am glad it is growing dusk."

"Why, mother dear?"

"You will not see my blushes or my tears."

CHAPTER IV.

MY MOTHER'S STORY.

THE reader must be weary of the everlasting ego of this simple biography, and it will be a relief to tell my mother's story in the third person. I have given it as a consecutive narrative—not as I should have written it down at the time, but with the fuller information and apprehension of womanhood.

There were many things an unsophisticated girl could not understand, and some things glossed over or entirely suppressed by my mother. But this is my mother's story, as she would have told it to a woman of her own age—as, in fact, she told it to Mrs. Annesley during the first days of her sojourn at the keeper's cottage, with some additional facts picked up later from others.

My mother was by birth half English, half Italian. Her father, Captain Ponsonby, was a cadet of an old North country family. Disgusted with the slow promotion in the Royal Navy, he left the service, and, possessed of a small private fortune, set out upon his travels. He had seen enough of the ocean. He wished now to become better acquainted with the land. He wandered from city to city, leaving each in turn when time began to hang heavily on his hands. Crossing Alps and Apennines, he found himself in Florence. He never travelled further south. There the days were always too short. He never lacked occupation and amusement. Every thing he desired was concentrated in the City of the Flowers. Nature was lavish with her beauty. The streets were galleries

of art. Life was a pleasure under such a
sun, and living was cheap enough to suit
his limited means.

A man sociably inclined, as was Kit
Ponsonby, found the cosmopolitanism of
Florence to his taste. He was a welcome
guest in the palaces of the old Italian
nobility, and in the saloons of English
and other visitors. Sometimes Kit talked
of running home for a London season; but
when it came to the point, he could never
tear himself away from the land of his
adoption. He preferred the Cascine Gardens
to Hyde Park, the Via Tornabuoni to Pall
Mall, and found a charm about the golden
Arno which did not exist in the silver
Thames, as he had heard it called, but
never knew why.

By natural evolution he lost his English habits and developed into a thorough
Florentine. Quick at catching a language,
his Italian became as good as his English;
indeed, in time better, as he practised the

one more than the other, and increased fluency in his adopted tongue was accompanied by hesitation in his own.

He had always been a joyous, light-hearted sailor, and his heart lost nothing of its lightness amongst the olives and the vines. He was gay, single, heart whole, jeering at all friends who were fools enough to place the matrimonial noose round their bachelor necks. But Love will have his revenge, and makes those who dispute his power the most abject of his slaves.

Kit Ponsonby met his fate in the person of a very beautiful girl, the only child of a widowed marchesa, whose whole fortune consisted of a palazzo in the Via Borgo Santi Apostoli. She lived with her daugh-. ter on the top story, and on the income derived from letting the lower flats. The marchesa was poor but proud, and pretended that she preferred rooms under the leads with the airy *loggia* attached, on account of the pure air and extensive view;

but the world knew she would gladly have inhabited the lofty saloons of the *primo piano*, if she could have afforded to forego their rent.

She had a real talent for music, and had been a fine performer on the piano. The talent was transmitted in a much more developed form to the daughter, who had also inherited her mother's beauty.

Kit Ponsonby made the acquaintance of the lovely Beatrice, or Bice, Castracane, at the house of a mutual friend, and succumbed at once to the charms of that sweet young face and sweeter voice. Though by no means a good *parti*, he made himself acceptable to the mother as well as the daughter, and before many weeks were over the gayest of bachelors was the most devoted of Benedicts.

It was Kit's turn now to be the laughing stock of his former friends; but with the loveliest woman in Florence for his wife, he could afford to treat their gibes with the contempt they deserved. But, alas! his happiness was not to be long-lived. His young wife died in giving birth to a girl, who was christened Beatrice, after her dead mother. Kit Ponsonby never smiled again. His bachelor friends tried to lure him back to his old ways, but gave it up when they found that he was no longer a boon companion. The poor fellow took to solitary drinking to drown his sorrow, which resulted in an early death, when his little daughter was only four years old.

The marchesa found herself much in the same position as before her daughter's marriage—she had a granddaughter to bring up instead of a daughter to bring out. Bice at a very early age began to show signs of extraordinary musical talent, which was cultivated by her grandmother as far as her knowledge went; but the girl soon wanted more advanced instruction, and this, fortunately, came to her unsought.

The marchesa had let a small apartment on the same flat which she inhabited to an artist of local celebrity. Luigi Tagliano was first violin at the Pergola Theatre, and a profound musician. He was attracted by Bice's sweet voice, which floated out of the marchesa's window and in at his own. The child picked up every air she heard, and if she could not find the words, she made words herself for the tune. Tagliano often saw her sitting at the window of her little schoolroom, which opened on the same gallery as his own window, and the two smiled themselves into a silent acquaintance, which soon became a speaking one. She told him how she loved music, and the difficulty she found in making progress without teaching. He offered to become her master, and told her to ask the marchesa permission for a daily lesson. The marchesa was delighted at the idea, and still more so, when the first violin insisted that the

lessons should be gratis. He told her that
he was captivated with the beautiful voice
and lovely face of her little granddaughter,
and that, having no child of his own, he
felt that the little Bice would be the joy
of his life, and that it would be a labour
of love to impart his musical knowledge
to her.

He took the child to his heart, and her
education became the purpose of his life.
The marchesa, grateful for the affection
lavished on her granddaughter and the
musical advantages offered at the same
time, forgot the social distinction in rank
between herself and the violinist, and received him on the most friendly terms, and
as time went on he was treated as Bice's
adopted father, and spent more hours in the
marchesa's apartment than in his own.
The girl gave him even more affection
than her grandmother, and the master took
as much pleasure in teaching as the pupil
in being taught.

Tagliano had special qualifications for training a voice, as in his early days he had been accompanyist to one of the greatest maestros in Italy, and had naturally a perfect knowledge of his method. It was not wonderful, then, that a girl with real musical genius should make rapid progress under such instruction. He was able, too, to give her another advantage not to be despised in a musical education. She had the privilege of hearing every singer of celebrity who came to Florence, it being the practice of Tagliano to place his adopted daughter in a corner of the orchestra, where the beautiful child was as well known by sight to the *habitués* of the Pergola as the first violin himself. When she became too old to accompany him to the orchestra, he was always able tó procure seats for her and the marchesa in the theatre. Bice seldom missed a rehearsal or a performance, so that she grew up almost in the theatre, and looked forward to the day when she might herself tread the boards. On her return from the opera, she was accustomed to criticize the singers, and discuss their good and bad points with her adopted father, who, in the morning, made her sing over the soprano parts, and imitate the one and avoid the other.

With such extraordinary advantages, it was not surprising that Beatrice Ponsonby, at the age of sixteen, was a finished singer. Her voice, though not at its fullest power, was a magnificent organ under perfect control, whilst the brilliancy of her execution was only equalled by the pathos and expression she was able to throw into the music. Her method was, of course, beyond criticism, as it was that of the greatest authority of the century.

The first violin had very great difficulty in persuading the marchesa to allow Bice to take to the stage as a profession, but ultimately she was induced to sacrifice her family pride by the prospect of the golden harvest to be reaped by such a voice. Beatrice had now acquired all that Tagliano could impart, but there was still much to be learned before she could appear before the footlights. She must study the technical part of the theatrical profession under a *maestro di declamazione*, as she would be called upon to act as well as sing. The first master of this class was attached to the Scala at Milan, and Tagliano resolved that his adopted daughter should become his pupil, and no other's.

The marchesa could not be persuaded to leave Florence, and arrangements were therefore made by the first violin that Beatrice should be received into the maestro's family for a year's training. All expenses were to be paid by himself, out of his savings. To this Beatrice strongly objected, as she thought the allowance made to the marchesa by the trustees of her father's small fortune should be utilized for this part of her theatrical education;

but Tagliano would not hear of it. She was his adopted daughter, he said, and all that was his would be hers some day. The marchesa's pride did not intervene, so Beatrice had to put her own pride in her pocket, and accept the liberality of her art-father with grateful thanks and a secret resolution to repay the money, when her notes became as negotiable as those of a bank.

Tagliano escorted his beloved pupil to Milan, and left her in the charge of the maestro's wife, who promised to be a mother to her and watch over her as if she were her own child. Tagliano might have kept the money he spent on the Cashmere shawl with which he presented her, for all the trouble she took to look after her charge! She saw her well fed and well clothed, and thought that that was all her promises entailed on her.

Amongst the visitors received at the house of the maestro was an American, one Joshua Hall, who, from the reckless manner with which he threw his money about, was accounted a millionaire. He was captivated by the great beauty of Beatrice Ponsonby, and made all the other *debutantes* jealous by the attentions he paid her and the costly presents he loaded her with. Beatrice was young and inexperienced, and accepted his gifts thoughtlessly, as a child accepts a doll. She had no idea that the giver expected to be taken with his gifts, and was profoundly astonished when he informed her that she had encouraged him to hope that she would accept him for a husband. She did not love the man, but was flattered by his attentions and proposal, and, with the perversity of a child, promised to be his wife, laughing at the idea of disgusted rivals, and dreaming of the endless amusement to be got out of her husband's long purse. She was surprised and annoyed when the American insisted on his proposal being kept secret, and subsequently married her privately.

The deed once done, she repented immediately. It was too late now to untie the knot. She longed to tell her adopted father of the step she had taken, but she did not dare to do so. Her husband was vulgar, intolerant, selfish, without one redeeming good quality; he threatened her life if she divulged the marriage, and treated her like the ruffian that he was. His fortune was a farce. He was a gambler, and spent his money freely when he was in funds; but since he had married Beatrice Ponsonby, his luck had deserted him, and his one aim was to turn his wife's talents into cash. He urged her to hasten her *début*. This she had the courage to refuse, saying that she left all professional matters to her masters.

There was not a more miserable girl than Beatrice. She grew careless in her studies. Her voice lost much of its beauty from the mental worry she underwent. She complained of illness, which her looks corroborated. She begged to be allowed to return to Florence for the benefit of her health, and had made every arrangements for doing so when, to the surprise of her maestro and his wife, she announced that she had changed her mind. With a bright face and cheerful voice, she begged to be allowed to continue her operatic and theatrical studies, which she did at once with renewed energy and success.

This complete *volte-face* was caused by the sudden departure of her husband. He confessed that he had spent all he possessed, and was obliged to run from his creditors. His love for his beautiful wife was only a passing fancy, which vanished with possession. Beatrice was delighted to be free, even temporarily, of so bad a husband, and it was not surprising that she received the news of his death without sorrow. The ship on which he had taken his passage

to America went down with all on board
in mid-Atlantic, and to make assurance
more sure the papers published the name
of Joshua Hall as being one of those
drowned.

Beatrice was now entirely free, and
relieved of the fear of her marriage being
found out. The silly girl had learned a
lesson which changed her character, or
rather improved what was naturally an
exceptionally honest, loving, and noble
character, by expunging the frivolous part,
attributable chiefly to the ignorance, in-
experience, and vanity of youth, and in
some degree to an Italian girl's want of
moral education. She was a woman now
—a self-contained woman, with powers of
intellect and strength of will sharpened
by the experience of life. She would not
again lend an ear to a flatterer's tale.
She had had enough of love-making
and matrimony. Art should now be her
only spouse, and to that spouse she gave

a heart's devotion. Her master was astounded at her progress as an actress. She took to the stage as a duck to water. Her acting was a revelation. She posed like a statue, and yet with such natural grace that art concealed the art. She walked the boards as easily as the floor of her own room, and the absence of nervousness was as remarkable as the play of passion and playfulness at her command. She threw herself into each part with abandon, forgetting herself entirely in the character she represented. Prophecies of a great success were rife all over Milan, and her maestro had no difficulty in finding her an engagement.

The marchesa and Luigi Tagliano were delighted at the accounts they received of her wonderful talents. Little did they think that she had been married and become a widow since they had seen her beautiful face. The marchesa still refused to leave Florence, so that the first violin journeyed alone to Milan to take charge of his adopted daughter. He found his child had grown into a woman, and wondered that a year could have made so extraordinary a change. She was as loving as ever, but there was a depth of character he had not expected to find. He thought she was too calm, too self-possessed, and feared that there might be a reaction when she appeared before the footlights.

They travelled together to Oneglia, a small town on the Riviera di Ponente, some twenty miles from Genoa, where she was to make her *début* in Petrella's charming opera "La Contessa di Amalfi." Tagliano's mind was set at rest the moment the curtain drew up in that pretty little theatre by the sea. Beatrice came forward with a composure unusual in a *debutante*. Her voice did not betray the slightest nervousness; she felt that she was mistress of her part, and did not see any occasion to fear that she would forget a note or a gesture; her familiarity with the stage, gained by constant attendance at the Pergola, stood her in good stead. She took Tagliano by surprise, who was not prepared by such a finished performance, and the house by storm. She was called and recalled after every act, and the happy widow received the thunders of applause with a smiling grace that captivated all hearts. Her performances at Oneglia were a prolonged ovation, and she returned to the Palazzo Castracane a prima donna of the first order.

"You left me a child," remarked the marchesa, "and you are come home a woman. If the air of Milan has aged you so, it is a lucky thing I did not go with you. I should have looked a hundred, at least."

"I am nineteen, grandmother," Beatrice replied. " At that age one ought to be full grown ; " and she drew herself up with a saucy smile, borrowed from her unmarried days."

" There, I like to see you smile; it makes you young again. You are too old for your years, Bice mia! Age comes fast enough without going to meet it. I wish you had never gone to Milan."

" Wait till you hear me at the Pergola, grannie."

Beatrice had dropped the name of Ponsonby, thinking an English name might not be acceptable to Italians, and taken that of the first violin as her *nom de théâtre*. The name of Beatrice Tagliano became rapidly known in the theatrical world, and she was overwhelmed with offers of engagements from the directors of many of the smaller theatres—a *debutante*, however successful, never being invited to sing at the great theatres of Italy till her reputation is established. Beatrice left the choice of her engagements to her Milanese maestro, and, accompanied by her adopted father and her maid Teresa, sang in the first year of her career at half a dozen theatres and in as many operas, where her beauty and wonderful talents created a perfect *furore*.

At last she was offered an engagement at the Pergola, to the intense satisfaction of the first violin as well as her own. His fondest dreams were realized; his much-loved pupil was to appear on the stage of the theatre where he had for so many years led the orchestra. He as well as the Marchesa Castracane were such well-known characters in Florence, that the *début* of one so dear to both would have filled the house and secured a *succès d'estime*, even if there had been no previous triumphs to excite curiosity. She appeared as Amina in the " Sonnambula," and from the opening recitation, " Care Compagne," to the joyous finale, " Ah non giunge," she was applauded to the echo. She was called and recalled after each act, and the excitement at the conclusion of the opera was such as could only be witnessed in an Italian opera house. Beatrice was drowned in bouquets,.

the largest of which she kissed and handed to the first violin. This graceful act brought the house down again. There was not a heart that was not touched, not a hand that did not beat applause; ladies waved their handkerchiefs, men stood on the benches and shouted the name of La Tagliano till they were hoarse. When the curtain drew up for the sixth time, she came forward leaning on her adopted father's arm, who she insisted should share her triumph; and then, dropping it, ran forward to a stage-box, and kissed her grandmother.

The house was in tears. The tears of Italians are very near the surface; but there was a stolid Englishman in the stalls, who saw the stage through a mist in his eyes. Sir Lionel Dampier felt that he had met his fate, and that if he could not play Elvino to the Amina of Beatrice Tagliano, life would not be life for him. For the first time he knew that he had a heart, but he knew also that he had lost it. The handsome young Englishman, the pet of Florence society, found no difficulty in being presented to the *debutante*. At their first meeting his eyes had spoken his admiration, and Beatrice, though she had resolved never to listen to men's love-tales again, felt for the first time that she had found her master. All her resolutions fell to pieces before the respectful love he offered her.

The baronet knew his own mind. As soon as he had reason to think that Beatrice might be induced to listen to his suit, he went direct to the marchesa, and in a straightforward English way asked her permission to lay his fortune and his heart at her granddaughter's feet. He was clever enough to understand the marchesa's hesitation. With more delicacy than was necessary, he told her that he felt, in removing such a bright particular star from the stage, he was depriving her of a large income, and that she must allow him to make a settlement on her as well as her granddaughter. Such a practical appeal was not to be refused, and the Marchesa Castracane assured Sir Lionel Dampier that, apart from all pecuniary considerations, she could not desire a more thoroughly satisfactory marriage for her dear granddaughter.

Tagliano was not so easily won over. It was like tearing out his heart to ask him to relinquish the operatic triumph of his adopted child. The theatre was his world, and, having by his teaching and exertion raised her to the position of a queen of song, it did seem very hard that she should be carried off by an Englishman, who, like all his compatriots, had no soul for, or knowledge of, music, to shine in a sphere for which she was not educated, and where her musical talents would not be appreciated. Sir Lionel made no attempt to purchase his consent. He knew that the first violin would have

been insulted by any proposition such as
had been tacitly accepted by the marchesa.
He felt that Tagliano loved his adopted
daughter too unselfishly to stand long in
the way of her happiness.

Beatrice was as deeply in love with
Sir Lionel as he with her. She gave
him her whole heart, and was ready to
forego the pleasant excitement of a triumphant operatic career to be his loved and
honoured wife. She knew he was wealthy,
she knew he came of an ancient family,
she knew that she was the envy of all the
unmarried girls in Florence, where he was
the great *parti* of the year; but she was
led by no sordid feelings, no satisfied vanity
to accept him as her husband. She loved
him for himself, for his warm heart, his
respectful adoration, his *chevalresque* character, his handsome face, and his noble
bearing. It was a true English love match,
where love was on both sides—love deep
and true and tender.

The first violin implored Beatrice not
to leave the stage in such a hurry. He
reminded her that she was depriving him
of all he had so long worked for, and that
she was taking the whole joy out of his
life. Beatrice felt the truth of his words,
and that she owed him a debt of gratitude
which she could never repay. She there
and then promised to defer her marriage
for a year, and give him the satisfaction
of seeing her continue her triumphs on
the stage for that period. Sir Lionel
Dampier could not disapprove of her com-
promise, but insisted that the marriage
should take place at once, in order that
he might be her protector on her operatic
tour.

Beatrice Ponsonby was married to Sir
Lionel Dampier both at the Embassy Chapel
and at the church of Or San Michele. All
Florence, fashionable and artistic, were
present at the wedding; and though some
shook their heads at the marriage of an

English baronet to an opera-singer, all
agreed that a handsomer couple never knelt
at the altar, or one where real old-fashioned
love was so evidently mutual. The happiness of Sir Lionel was complete, as he
started with his beautiful bride to spend
a short honeymoon at the baths of Lucca.
She looked as radiantly happy as she
was beautiful. She had only one regret,
that she had not the courage to tell her
husband of her previous marriage. She
felt that she had done wrong in concealing
it, but it was too late now to rectify her
error.

CHAPTER V.

MY MOTHER'S STORY (*continued*).

THE honeymoon was short, as the bride was engaged to sing three weeks after her marriage at the Fenice, at Venice. Sir Lionel naturally did not quite like the part of husband to a prima donna, but he effaced himself with a good grace. The gratitude of his wife and the delight of the first violin, who joined them at Venice, made up in some measure for the false position into which love had brought him.

At the end of a year of operatic triumphs, Sir Lionel carried his wife off to England, and proudly introduced her to his beautiful ancestral home. She was delighted with everything she saw, and would have settled down at once as the proud and happy mistress of Beechover Hall had it not been for the presence of her mother-in-law.

The Dowager Lady Dampier was externally a charming woman, fresh and young for her fifty years. She had been very beautiful, and still retained her good looks, but did not pretend to be younger than she was. She left nature to itself, and used no cosmetics to hide the few wrinkles with which her face was marked. Her cheeks were pink with the ripe look of a russet apple, and her hair was still plentiful, though grey. She was still very handsome, and considered by many as good as she was handsome. Those who knew her well knew better. The Dowager was puritanical, proud, vindictive, and utterly unscrupulous. She loved her son, but the tigress also loves its whelps.

She had other causes besides jealousy for hating her son's wife. She looked on the

stage as a sink of iniquity, and classed actors
and actresses with publicans and sinners; she
was, moreover, one of those narrow-minded
patriots who can see nothing good in a
foreigner. This Pharisee in petticoats had,
therefore, the double mortification of finding that her son had married an opera-
singer, and an Italian; for young Lady
Dampier had nothing English about her
beyond her name. The Dowager was more
provoked at this *mésalliance*, as she called
it, from the fact that she had made up her
mind that a daughter of the Duke of
Axminster, Lord Lieutenant of the county,
was to be her son's wife, and was assiduously
cultivating the connection; indeed, Lady
Grace Lawley was staying with her at the
time when she received the news of her
son's engagement. She had written her
feelings very strongly, and implored Sir
Lionel to pause before he disgraced the
family by such a low marriage. He
was not a man to alter his mind when

once made up, and the mother's angry words only increased his love for the beautiful girl she maligned.

Contrary to his expectation, on returning to England with his bride, he found the Dowager in possession of the hall. She had so long been the mistress of his house that she did not mean to resign her place without a struggle.

The Dowager received her daughter-in-law with studied coldness—a coldness which was meant to be felt, and contrasted strongly with the effusive affection lavished on her son. She repulsed the young bride when she came forward to be embraced, giving her the tips of her fingers, and addressing her as Lady Dampier. Beatrice broke into a fit of weeping when she found herself alone with her husband, and asked whether this was the sort of reception English mothers gave to their sons' wives. He tried to make excuses, saying that the Dowager was cold and formal, but

that she loved him too well not to extend her
love to his wife. He begged her for his
sake to put up for a time with his mother's
unmotherly treatment, and to endeavour
to thaw the ice with the sunny influence
of her beautiful eyes. Beatrice did her
best to ingratiate herself with her mother-
in-law and to win her regard; but without any success.

Sir Lionel, seeing the fruitless exertions
of his sweet wife, became very irritated,
and expressed himself strongly to his
mother. He went so far as to remind her
that the house was his, and that his wife
was its mistress. He had not, however,
the moral courage to insist that the Dowager
should find a new home for herself. He
had always been kept as a boy in complete subjection to her will, and as a man
found it difficult to emancipate himself from
the control of so intolerant a character.
He had, too, a strong filial feeling that
he ought not to banish his mother from

the home which had so long been her own.

After this angry interview with her son, the Dowager was more wary, and abstained in his presence from open rudeness to his wife; but when his back was turned, she heaped every petty persecution and insult on the poor bride. Once and again the Italian blood fired up, and the Dowager for a time was cowed into better behaviour. Beatrice, out of love for her husband, bore the cruel treatment without complaining, hoping that her mother-in-law's animosity would wear itself out. And a time came when it seemed that such was the case. The Dowager changed her tactics; she became officiously civil, and tried to worm herself into the confidence of her son's wife. She told her that past unkindness was caused by jealousy of the woman who had come between her and her son, and she now asked for forgiveness in such a humble manner that Beatrice almost believed her regret to be genuine. But the claws were only curled up under the velvet paws.

The London season took the family from Beechover Hall to Eaton Square. To Sir Lionel's great delight he saw that his mother and wife were apparently on the most friendly terms. The Dowager presented her daughter-in-law at an early drawing-room, and seemed pleased to accompany her into society. The young wife was flattered by the reception given to her beauty and talents. The Dowager encouraged her to enter into the very thick of the dissipations of London life, and ridiculed the fatigue she sometimes complained of. Beatrice became the acknowledged belle of the season. No party was perfect without her presence, and her own receptions were crowded with all the rank and fashion of society. She was a proud and happy woman; she had the entire love of her husband, and had con-

quered the aversion and jealousy of her
mother-in-law—at least, so she thought.
Sir Lionel worshipped his wife daily
more and more, and was delighted with
the popularity she had won by her wonderful singing and glorious beauty. The
prospects of an heir added to the happiness of both.

Sir Lionel, though the most sociable of
men, and never so happy as when surrounded by his friends, to whom he ex-
tended a princely hospitality, did not enjoy
London society. Hot rooms were his ab-
horrence, and late hours interfered with
his early ride, without which he could not
tolerate town life. For a time he accompanied his wife and mother on their evening round of engagements, as he was proud
of being the husband of the most beautiful
woman in the room, and enjoyed the sensation she created. But soon he begged
to be let off, and Lady Dampier, though
she missed him more than she liked to

confess, was not selfish enough to sacrifice his comfort to her own.

Beatrice, new to English life and London society, was, of course, ignorant of the characters and reputations of those with whom she mixed. She had to be guided in her selection of acquaintances by her mother-in-law, who introduced her, amongst others, to men of the most dissipated characters, and encouraged them to be frequent visitors at Eaton Square, especially at times when her son was not likely to be in the way. She then began to throw out hints amongst the greatest gossips of her acquaintance that her daughter-in-law was making intimacies with men of whom she disapproved, naming one or two of profligate as well as fashionable notoriety, whom she herself had thrown in her way. The innuendoes were handed on as facts. Young Lady Dampier's name began to be spoken lightly of, and society shrugged its shoulders, and asked what could be expected of an opera-singer.

The season came to a conclusion, and both
Sir Lionel and Lady Dampier were delighted to return to their beautiful country
place. Neither of them had the slightest
idea of the unpleasant rumours that were
in circulation. The Dowager, satisfied with
the result of her innuendoes, made herself
more agreeable than ever to her daughter-
in-law.

A succession of visitors kept the hall
gay during the autumn, and the Dowager
dropped her hints in the fertile soil of country
gossip as she had done in that of town.
There were not a happier married couple
than Sir Lionel and Lady Dampier; they
loved each other and lived for each other,
and the arrival of a little daughter in the
spring gave them an additional bond of
union, something more to love and live for.

Lady Dampier would gladly have given
up the season to remain with her husband
and child; and Sir Lionel, who never
wished to leave his country home, would

have been the last to press her to go to town. But a sudden vacancy in the seat for the county occurred just before Easter, and Sir Lionel, persuaded to stand on the Conservative side, was elected Member of Parliament by a large majority. There was now no getting out of a migration to Eaton Square.

The spirits of the Dowager, which had been depressed at the prospect of Sir Lionel and his wife staying in the country with baby, now rose as rapidly as they had fallen. She hoped to see her demoniacal efforts crowned with success. It would be harder to separate husband and wife now that they were brought closer together by the birth of a child, but her hatred and jealousy of Beatrice had grown in proportion to the husband's love for his wife, and she was prepared to work the ruin of her rival, or rather supplanter in her son's affection, at any cost. She continued the tactics she had found so far successful. She began by accompanying her daughter-in-law into society, and when she found that Beatrice was much admired by an Italian prince, she suddenly pleaded indisposition as an excuse for remaining at home, and told her gossips that she could not go about with a woman who in her flirtations outraged decency so openly.

Poor Lady Dampier had not the faintest idea that her name was coupled with that of Prince Bellarosa. She liked his society, as he spoke her native language and loved music. He possessed a delightful tenor voice, which had been well trained. They practised together, and constantly sang duets in society. They were thus thrown together, which gave a certain colour to the slanders of the Dowager. Young Lady Dampier wondered sometimes why people looked shyly at her, who had been friendly before. Her parties were not so crowded, and one or two ladies had absolutely cut her. She spoke openly of all this to her husband, who only laughed at what he called her fancies.

The Dowager was delighted, and took a step forward. She began to hint to Sir Lionel that he had better look after his wife, who was said to be a great deal too much with the Italian prince. Annoyed beyond measure at such a suggestion, he told his mother never to bring him any gossip of that sort, at the same time begging her, if she could detect any one spreading such a report, to let him know the name, and he would settle with the slander-monger. Confident of the faithful love of his wife, the next moment he forgot all about the matter, and not a suspicion clouded his perfect content as he played with the child smiling on its proud mother's lap. It was hard to say which was happiest or proudest, Sir Lionel or his wife.

All of a sudden everything was changed. Lady Dampier became low and depressed. She was never heard laughing with her baby girl; her husband missed her sunny smile; she seemed to avoid his glance and shrink from his touch. In society, she was no longer the gay beauty. She looked a weary, tired woman. The colour faded from her cheek, the lustre from her eye. Sir Lionel began to be anxious, thinking that his wife must be seriously ill. He implored her to take advice; but though she promised to see Sir William Jenner, she never kept her word. She tried in her husband's presence to force a spurious kind of gaiety, but it was a very poor imitation. More than once he caught her weeping by her bady's cradle. She could give no reason for her tears, except that she was out of spirits. When he tried to kiss her spirits back, she gazed up into his eyes with a strange yearning look of love, and then turned away with a sudden shudder. He could not make it out, but he loved her none the less; and as for doubting her, a doubt never crossed his mind!

The Dowager saw the change with in-
finite pleasure. She felt her work was
nearly over, and that soon she would be
rewarded with having her son all to herself.
When the wife was gone, the mother would
recover the love that had been robbed from
her. She put her own interpretation on the
depressed state of Lady Dampier's spirits.
The wish was father to the thought. She
made up her mind that her daughter-in-law
was a faithless wife, and that she was
ashamed to meet the look of the husband
she had deceived.

It seemed to the Dowager to be too good to
be true; she hardly expected to have secured
her object so soon. But so confident was
she that her view was correct, that she went
to a private inquiry office, and gave directions that young Lady Dampier should be
watched, and her movements reported to her.

The news brought her was most exhila-
rating. The pink cheeks of the Dowager
flushed with the certainty of coming vic-

tory. She felt like a general who, after laying down an elaborate plan of sieging operations, saw each outwork falling exactly as he had arranged. The last mine was about to be sprung, and the enemy would be at her mercy. God help the man or woman who found him or herself at the mercy of the Dowager Lady Dampier!

The detectives belonging to the inquiry office, that most un-English of modern innovations, reported that Lady Dampier was in the habit of leaving her house in Eaton Square, quietly dressed, and with a thick veil over her face, and walking through Chester Square over Ecclestone Bridge to a street in Pimlico, not bearing a high character for the morality of its inhabitants. She was evidently expected at one of the small houses, as a man on the look-out from the dining-room window let her in without ringing. She had been tracked three times to the same house.

The Dowager was jubilant. She would,

in a few days, be sole mistress of her son's home and heart! She never thought that the home might be deserted and the heart broken. She was much more in awe of her son than she used to be. Her insinuations against his wife had widened the breach between them, and his eyes had flashed with an intensity of anger of which she had not thought his quiet nature capable. She did not dare tell him of the employment of detectives and their discoveries. She, therefore, stooped to the usual medium of communication in favour with cowards and mean souls—an anonymous letter, which gave the address of the house in Pimlico visited by Lady Dampier. Sir Lionel's first impulse was to tear the letter up; but, remembering his mother's hints, he showed it to her. She affected the greatest surprise, and hoped things had not gone so far. She again repeated the scandals that were afloat respecting Lady Dampier and the Italian

prince, and advised him, for his own satisfaction, to watch his wife. If nothing
came of it, it would only be another instance
of a lie propagated anonymously.

Sir Lionel followed his mother's advice,
and followed his wife one morning. To
his dismay and bitter anguish he saw her
enter the house indicated. He felt stabbed
to the heart. To think that the woman
whom he loved so tenderly, and who
he thought returned his love so fully,
should deceive him so foully! Stunned by
the agonizing severity of the blow to all
his happiness, he held on for a moment to
some area railings, and then crept, poor
heart-broken Sir Lionel, to the further
end of the street to wait for her exit. He
waited an hour, with feelings that it would
be profane to attempt to describe. His
faith in God and man was gone. He stood
there like his own ghost, looking down on
a dead life, hopeless, loveless, a prey to an
abject despair.

When Lady Dampier came out, she was
accompanied by a man, who left her in
the Buckingham Road and went off in the
direction of Victoria Station. He saw it
was not the prince. Sir Lionel followed
his wife home and up to her room. An
agonizing scene followed, in which Sir
Lionel accused his wife of shameless conduct. The poor woman fell on her knees,
buried her face in her hands, and was silent.
He told her to leave his house at once and
for ever. She rose, and walked quietly
into the nursery, followed by her husband.
She knelt down by the side of the child's
cradle, kissed its sleeping eyes, and dropped
a tear upon its rosy cheeks. She then left
the room, and went downstairs, slowly,
humbly, silently. There was no one in
the hall. She walked to the door. Sir
Lionel was close behind her in a waking
dream of lost hopes, lost love, lost life.
She turned, threw her arms round his neck,
gave him a long last parting kiss, and was

gone. The kiss seemed to burn upon his cheek. He never forgot it. There was such a depth of love in it that it seemed hard to believe it to be the kiss of a faithless wife.

Sir Lionel was persuaded to apply for a divorce, and, the case being undefended, obtained a decree *nisi*.

The victorious Dowager, not satisfied with having got rid of the wife, persuaded her son, by inventing all sorts of scandalous stories which could not now be contradicted, that he was not the father of the child, and obtained permission to send it away out of his sight. But she did not find that the absence of wife and child had any effect in bringing back her son's affection to his mother. On the contrary, she saw that he only tolerated her presence. He did not tell her that he had discovered not only that she was the employer of the detectives, and the writer of the anonymous letter, but that she had pur-

posely placed temptation in his wife's way.
In fact, he believed that the whole train
of circumstances which led up to his
divorce had been planned by her. He did
not dare question her on the subject, as he
feared he might be carried away by righteous indignation, and curse the mother who
bore him. He wished to avoid this, but
he none the less looked on her with loathing and disgust, and left his home and
country without wishing her good-bye.

Sir Lionel, alone in the world, worse
than motherless, wifeless, childless, went
abroad, and endeavoured to drown the
anguish of his heart in the excitement of
wild sports, in which he was sometimes
joined by a young friend, Lord Glanmire,
the only creature whose company he could
tolerate. Now and then he paid a flying
visit to England, when business absolutely
required it. On these occasions he declined
to see his mother. Beechover Hall was
closed, and the Dowager lived in Eaton

Square, where she kept up an appearance
of a virtuous life, being constant in her
attendance at church, and much given to
acts of open charity. She showed herself
at Court, and went into society. Poor(?)
Lady Dampier was much respected, and
looked upon as an example of Christian
resignation under heavy trials. Her looks
were so pleasant and her complexion so
clear that it was impossible to think she
could possess a bad heart or suffer from
indigestion. She did suffer fearfully,
though it may not have been from bodily
illness. She was alone with her sin, which
was punishment enough in this world. It
was only her maid who knew her real
character, and saw her in her paroxyms of
fury and remorse. She had to be well
paid for waiting on a demon.

Sir Lionel never really ceased to love his
wife; he tried to hate her, but could only
think of her with affection. He did not
inquire what had become of her; he wished

to be ignorant of her whereabouts, lest he should be constrained to find her out. He had given his lawyers instructions to trace her, and to see that she was provided with an income—an income which she refused to touch.

His friend Lord Glanmire wished to lure him back from his wandering life and see him settled again, with another wife, in the home of his ancestors. But Sir Lionel was not to be lured into forgetfulness of the past. In African forests, on Norway fiords, on North American prairies, he was always haunted by the eyes of his beautiful wife as she gazed at him for the last time, before she fled from her home, and by the memory of the passionate kiss, which somehow seemed to him to have been one more of love than penitence.

If he only could have known the truth, he would have found that there was no penitence in that last embrace. His wife had nothing to repent of. All the stories of her flirtations were the pure inventions of that wicked woman, though her strangely depressed spirits gave them a colour of truth.

In the height of her popularity a bitter trouble fell on Lady Dampier—a trouble that would have killed a weaker woman, as it was the death-blow to her happiness. She received a letter, with an American postmark. She opened it at the breakfast table, and thrust it into her pocket. The signature was " Your affectionate husband, Joshua Hall." It required strong nerves to read such tidings without fainting away. The Dowager saw that something was wrong, and, with affected kindness, asked if she felt ill, as her face was so white. Sir Lionel looked up anxiously, but was satisfied by his wife's assurance that she was perfectly well. She retired to her room the moment she was able to escape, and read the appalling letter, which announced not only that her husband had not been a passenger in the ill-fated ship in which he was supposed

to have been drowned, but that he would
be in England almost as soon as his letter.
Whether he claimed her or not depended
on herself. He did not care sufficiently for
her society to insist on his marital rights.
He had been unfortunate in America (a
euphemism for imprisonment for robbery),
and saw no other way of keeping body and
soul together than by appealing to his wife
for funds. What was the good of having
a rich wife if she did not support her
husband?

Lady Dampier at first thought of telling
Sir Lionel the whole truth, but she feared
that it would break his heart, as she knew
how great and unselfish was the love he
bore her. She put off doing so from day
to day, hoping that some accident might
keep Joshua Hall in America.

A second letter, however, reached her
ten days later, saying that her husband
had arrived in London, and wished to see
her at once. She obeyed the summons,

and took with her all the jewels she could call her own, with the view of buying his silence till she could see her duty more clearly. She felt that not being Sir Lionel's wife, she had no right to remain under his roof. The conflict between love and duty was terrible. Had she only herself to think of, she would probably have left Sir Lionel, and returned at once to her grandmother at Florence. But her love was so great that she thought more of his feelings than her own. She was sure that he would never let her leave him, and would pay the American well to take himself off. But could she allow this ? Could she remain with a man who was not legally her husband ? It was a bitter struggle ; but the more she thought, the more she felt that the bond between herself and Sir Lionel must be severed sooner or later ; and the only question was, how to sever it with the least pain to the man who loved her so dearly ?

She paid several visits to her American husband, each time taking what money she could scrape together from the sale of valuables that were her own property, putting off the evil day, when she would have to break a good man's heart, her own being already well-nigh broken. She had made up her mind that this was the last time she would see Joshua Hall; she was going to tell him that he need not look for anything more from her, and that he would gain nothing by applying to Sir Lionel Dampier, as she was about to reveal the whole truth to him, and then leave him for ever. It was on this occasion that Sir Lionel followed her, and waited in the street while she told the American her resolution.

She was happier when she went up to her room than she had been for many days, as she had determined to do her duty, and felt that anything was better than the agonizing suspense and uncertainty as to what action she should take. She had removed her thick veil, and was going to make up her mind when and how she would break the terrible news to her husband, who was no longer her husband, when Sir Lionel came into the room. She knew by his face that he had discovered something, but was not prepared for his accusations of infidelity.

It suddenly flushed through her brain that it would be better for her husband, if not for herself, that she should not deny the imputation. If he knew the truth, he would not love her less, perhaps love her more, and would use all the influence of his great love to keep her with him. She feared she could not stand against so great a temptation. She thought, too, that if he looked on her as vile and shameless, his love might turn to hate; and, out of the deep love she bore him, she would rather that he despised her as a worthless creature than cherish hopeless love for one who

could no longer be his wife. The love
must be rooted out of his heart. The
operation would be a cruel one, but for his
dear sake she would help to tear up by
the roots the love that was her pride, her
life, her all.

Such self-sacrifice may appear foolishly
quixotic to cold English eyes, but Beatrice
was an Italian, impulsive and emotional, and
loved with the intense passion of the South.
Only a brave and noble woman could have
left the two beings she loved more than
herself—her husband and her child—as she
left them. There was no guilt in those
weeping eyes, nothing but love—love unutterable, as she went out, carrying a
breaking heart into the heartless streets of
London.

The outcast from her home walked
straight to Victoria Station, and took the
first train to Dover. She, fortunately, had
retained sufficient money to carry her to
Florence, where she arrived weary, deso-

late, and penniless; she crept up the many stairs which led to her grandmother's door. With eyes preternaturally large and bright, and hands hot as burning coals, she threw herself upon the marchesa's neck, and then sank, apparently lifeless, to the ground. The first violin was called at once, but Beatrice did not recognize her old master's voice. He carried her to her room, and laid her on the bed where she had slept so many guileless years. She lay there unconscious weary days and nights, prostrate with brain fever. In her delirium, she constantly talked of two husbands— one hated, and one dearly loved.

Tagliano wrote to Sir Lionel, stating that his wife had reached Florence, and was lying in a desperate fever. He asked for an explanation of the circumstances under which she had left her home with nothing but the clothes upon her back. The only answer he received was a copy of the *Times*, containing the notice of

Sir Lionel Dampier's application for a divorce.

After my mother awoke to consciousness, no allusion was made to the past. She went back to her old habits as if they had never been interrupted. As health slowly returned, she began to take some interest in her Florentine surroundings. She asked after old friends, and what opera was being given at the Pergola. She began to sing a little, and talked of some day returning to the stage. The marchesa and Tagliano both thought that the last two years had slipped out of her memory, that her mind was a blank as to the events that had occurred during that period; but when Beatrice found that some who had been friendly looked coolly on her now, she asked her grandmother what reports existed about her in Florence. She heard, without astonishment, that her husband had divorced her. She now understood the cold reception she had met with.

She could put up with the treatment from
former friends, but could not bear that her
grandmother and adopted father should
think that she had sinned, and, under promises of strict secresy, told them the whole
of her painful story. They pressed her
to let the truth be told, at all events, in
Florence; but she persisted in refusing, as
she preferred to be judged wrongly than
that the man she had injured unwittingly
should learn that she was not guilty, and
should give her back his love. She had
his hate, and wished to keep it; it was
better for him—better for her.

She returned everything that had been
sent after her—clothes, jewels, everything
that had not belonged to her before she
married Sir Lionel, and refused the generous
allowance which she was informed would
be placed quarterly to her credit at the
bank of Fenzi & Co.

Wishing to add to the marchesa's and
her own small income, as well as to divert

her mind from her troubles, she appeared again on the stage, changing her *nom de théâtre* from Tagliano to Bardi. She had now no thought but her art, and her reputation as a singer and an actress soon became the talk of music-loving Italy. In parts where passion and pathos were required, Beatrice Bardi was unsurpassed. In "Lucia di Lammermoor" and "La Forza del Destin" she was superb. She continued her career on the Lyric stage with triumph and success. Addresses, flowers, jewels, torchlight serenades followed La Bardi wherever she sang. She accepted their attentions gracefully and gratefully, but her smiles were only a part of her acting. Her heart was far away, with the only man she ever loved, and loved all the more since she had ruined his life.

Her American husband, after a time, found out that La Bardi and La Tagliano were one and the same person, and came

to claim his wife, or a compensatory income
for keeping out of her way. She agreed
to make him an allowance on the understanding that he should never show himself in any place whilst she was singing
at the theatre; but this did not entirely
free her from occasional visits at Florence,
when he tried by threats and prayers to
extort something over and above the
allowance.

La Bardi had worked at her profession
so diligently and conscientiously for over
fifteen years, without taking sufficient rest,
that latterly her strength had somewhat
given way, and the doctor had ordered a
complete change of scene and entire repose
from the fatigues of the stage.

And so the prima donna came to England, as we have seen, and was enjoying
pure air and repose in breezy little Lyndhurst, where I found—what I had almost
despaired of finding—a singing mistress—
and a mother!

CHAPTER VI.

IN OUR SUMMER PALACE.

My grandmother's visit to the keeper's cottage was a flying one, but the results were not transient. It was the commencement of a new era in my life. I felt morally and physically changed. I was a child before, now I was a woman. I had tasted the fruit of the tree of knowledge of good and evil, and found it very bitter.

I had now to face the world and its troubles, but I had one consolation. I was free from the control of a demon whom I hated, and now only owed obedience to an angel whom I loved. I was to share a mother's joys and sorrows; not that there was much prospect of happiness for her, but to ease the burden she had to bear was happiness enough for me.

We had long consultations as to future plans, in which Mrs. Annesley often joined. She would have liked to have kept us with her, for a time at all events; but my mother said that her peaceful holiday must come to an end, as she must be thinking of making a provision for me, now that I was cast off by my father's family. As she could not expect her voice to last for ever, she must make hay while the sun shone. With the small income left her by her father, and the palazzo in the Via Borgo Santi Apostoli, both of which would be mine, there would always be enough to keep body and soul together. She had also laid by a nice little nest-egg from the savings of her professional career, on which she would almost have been contented to have retired. The nest-egg would have long ago swelled into a fortune if she had

accepted engagements in Paris and London,
but she had contented herself with the
comparatively small salary of a prima donna
in Italy, in order that she might keep out
of the sight of the man who had loved her,
and, as he had never married again, perhaps
loved her still. She had intended, before returning to Italy, to have spent a short time
in London, in the hope that, by hovering
about the door of Sir Lionel's home in Eaton
Square, she might have caught a passing
sight of her little Nellie; but now that she
had got a big Nellie all to herself, she proposed carrying me off at once with her,
in some measure actuated by the fear that
the Dowager might change her mind, and
separate her again from her child.

I looked on my mother's decision with
mingled pleasure and pain : pleasure that
I should be her constant companion, and, I
hoped, her comfort; pleasure that I should
see something of the world beyond the
boundaries of the beautiful forest, which I

had never overstepped for the five happy
years I had lived in the cottage by the
stream ; but pain—pain greater than words
could express—that I was to bid farewell
to dear, kind Mrs. Annesley, who had
mothered me so lovingly and taught me all
I knew, whose influence had ever been
for good, and the example of whose quiet
godly life had led me, I hoped, to emulate
some of her many Christian virtues ; pain
that I was leaving scenes I loved so well
—the green glades amongst the oaks and
beeches, the purple heather - lands, the
flower-spangled bogs, the little valleys
with their whispering rills, and the hills
with their vignette peeps of distant land-
scapes, or with wider panoramas over rolling forest and fertile plain.

But every other pain was swallowed up
in one, and that was parting with the companion of my childhood. How could I
leave England and Bertie ? He had been
my only playmate. He had been father,

mother, brother, friend, all in one. My love
for him had grown with my growth. I began
by loving him as a brother. I now knew
that I loved him with a very different love
—a woman's first love : strong, deep, and
overpowering. I knew that if it was my
first love, it was also my last. I felt that I
was not like other girls; my life had been
so different. I had never played with
other children, never made friendships with
other girls. Bertie was the one youthful
experience of my life; and what a sweet
experience it was! I could never have
found a better, truer friend, none more
gentle, none more strong ; not one in all
the world so beautiful, at least in my eye,
so proud and yet so humble, so masterful,
and yet so easily led by a look, if it came
from eyes he loved.

Oh, Bertie, how could I leave you ? I
cried myself to sleep, as I thought of the
great heaving piteous ocean which would
soon be rolling between us.

The day was fixed for our departure. I could not leave England without seeing him, whose image filled my heart. I dreaded saying farewell, and yet I must say it. I must see him, and let him know that in leaving him I was leaving my heart's best love behind me. It might be unmaidenly; but it would be unwomanly to go away without a word or sign that I loved him. If he loved me as I loved him, it would half break his heart. I knew that his affection for me was real; but was it the sort of love I bore him? Could he support a life in which I had no lot or share? Life without him would be a living death to me. That was the test. Did he love me with a brother's love, or something far more deep and strong? I was not quite sure. I thought he did. I could not leave without learning the truth. If he loved me in the way I hoped he did, I could go on my way rejoicing, with health and spirits to cheer my mother's bitter lot.

I should try and be the sunshine of her home, the consolation of her heart; for with Bertie to love me, life would be a hymn of praise, a melody without an end. But if it were not so, if he only loved me as a sister, I did not dare to think of the future. Even a mother's love could not lead me through such a hopeless life. I had her example for bearing a far heavier lot; but, then, I did not possess her strength of character, her abnegation of self, her nobility of soul.

Bertie was in London with his uncle, who had come home unexpectedly from India, and had sent for him from his French studio. I could, of course, have seen him as we passed through town on our way to the South, but I did not care to see him in my mother's presence. She had not belonged to our forest days, and could not understand the intimacy between us; and, besides, if I could not be alone in his company, I could not use my woman's wits to take the gauge of his love for me.

I must have him all to myself for a little space before I left England, perhaps for years, perhaps for ever. So I wrote and told him that I could not leave the New Forest without wishing him farewell. I begged him to come down one day before our departure by an early train, and that I would meet him at one of our favourite spots—our Summer Palace, we called it. We would picnic, he and I, under the beeches, and spend one last day together in the recesses of the forest we both loved so well.

Bertie was delighted with my idea, and fixed an early day. I was only to bring fresh lettuces, with cream and eggs for the salad dressing, and some strawberries. Our last meal together, he said, must be one to be remembered, and he would try and make it memorable by the delicacies he provided. Oh! unromantic Bertie, to think of indulging our palates, when I only wished to satisfy the craving of my heart!

I paid special attention to my toilette on the morning of our day of meeting. I dressed my hair after a new fashion, taught me by my mother. Bertie had only seen it hanging in long golden curls over my shoulders. I hoped he would observe the change, and understand that I was grown up. I wore a pretty white frock, on which I fastened a spray of dark damask roses for a shoulder knot; a couple of the same roses I stuck coquettishly in the ribbon of my broad leghorn hat. My glass told me that I was looking my best. I was glad to be so pretty, because it pleased the eyes of those I loved.

I had never known any girls of my own age, to teach me their little conceits and tricks to attract attention; all the fascination I possessed was spontaneous, and I meant to exercise it on Bertie to-day. I was no flirt, only a guileless maiden, with a heart full of one great love, and a desire that it should be returned.

I was obliged to let Mrs. Nutburn into my secret, as without her help I could not have obtained the cream and the eggs for my salad. She packed my basket herself, adding, as a present to Bertie, a cold chicken and some cakes, for which he had a special weakness. Leaving her to make excuses for my absence from the early dinner, I crept out by the back way, and was soon flitting through the chequered shadows of the forest, a basket in one hand, a crimson parasol in the other.

Our rendezvous was a couple of miles off, in the direction of Brockenhurst, where Bertie was to leave the train. I was the first to arrive. It was an ideal trysting-place. The interwoven branches of the old beeches were the rafters of our Summer Palace, their foliage the tiles, and the straight grey stems inlaid with moss and lichens the columns. The ground sloped down to a forest stream, whose banks were green with nodding fern fronds and tangles of honeysuckle and wild rose. My throne, as Bertie called it, was at the base of a gigantic beech, whose moss-grown trunk formed the back, and two outstretching roots the arms. There was room enough for two upon my throne, but Bertie had always sat below, where a thick root divided into two, and made him a comfortable chair. Here we had passed many a happy summer day.

I sat down and fell a-dreaming—Bertie the centre figure in all my dreams. He loved me, and would bring me back some day to a beautiful home in my own dear forest, where our two mothers should be our guests, and—

"Asleep, Nellie?" cried a well-known voice, calling me back from dreamland. "Just fancy, not hearing my footsteps on the dry leaves!"

I looked round, and there was Bertie,

leading a forest pony. "Not asleep, but dreaming," I answered, jumping up, my cheeks rosy with joy at seeing my dear companion. I gave him my hand. He held it tight, and looked at me steadfastly, surprised and pleased. I blushed scarlet under his gaze. We were no longer boy and girl. I was a woman, and he had grown into a man—tall, broad-shouldered. The long moustache made such a difference in his handsome face, but the eyes were the same—the dear old eyes that had watched over me all the happy years I had lived under the shadow of the oaks and beeches.

"Dreaming!" he exclaimed—"dreaming of all the beautiful things you are to see, and the gay life you are going to lead, in the sunny South!"

"I do not think I shall ever be quite happy away from the New Forest. I should never wish to leave it, if it were not for my mother;" and the tears came into my eyes at the thought of going away from it—and Bertie.

" I thought all girls liked change, Nellie ? "

" I dare say some do. I don't like leaving old friends. What shall I do without your mother, Bertie ? "

" You have got a mother of your own now, Nellie. You surely can do without mine ! "

" Indeed, I can't. Think what she has been to me all these years ! "

" You would not like to rob me of my mother? But perhaps a way might be found of sharing her with you."

" Do tell me how that could be managed, Bertie ? "

" You are too inquisitive, Miss Dampier. How you have grown since I saw you six months ago ! "

" I am a woman now ; " and I drew myself up to my full height.

" How old are you, Nellie ? "

" Eighteen, and you are twenty."

"What an old couple we are!" said Bertie, laughing. " So you really are going to leave us with this new-born mother of yours. I hear she is a paragon of perfection. Mammie raves about her."

" She is very sweet and very beautiful."

" As beautiful as you, Nellie?" he asked. It was the first time he had ever paid me a compliment.

" A thousand times more so."

"I never saw any one so lovely as you are to-day! You have changed a great deal, Nellie!"

" Then you thought me plain before! a sort of ugly duckling."

" You were always a pretty child, but now you are a beautiful woman."

" Really, Bertie, I think you have changed more than I have. You have learned to flatter. Come and help me unpack your hamper, and don't talk any more nonsense."

I laid the cloth on the stump of a
felled tree, and arranged the table for our
tête-à-tête dinner, whilst Bertie dressed the
salad. I had brought some roses for
decoration and a button-hole, which I
placed by Bertie's plate. On the ground I
laid another cloth, and placed on it my cold
chicken, the cakes, and the strawberries.
Bertie then produced his contributions to
the feast—a beautiful lobster, a *terrine* of
foie gras, a box of *Marrons glacés*, and a
bottle of champagne.

We sat down to this sumptuous repast.
I had been very hungry before, but my
appetite seemed to have disappeared. I
trifled with the lobster and the salad. I
felt shy, for the first time, in Bertie's society.
He asked me why I did not eat like he did.
I blushed, and said that it was too hot to
take much food. Bertie opened the champagne, and made me drink a couple of
glasses. The wine restored my appetite,
and for a time we talked and laughed

away in the old familiar way. Dinner over, I retired with the strawberries and the *Marrons glacés* to my throne. Bertie took his armchair, and we commenced our dessert. Our conversation became very desultory, but we covered the pauses by picking at the fruit. Bertie was growing as shy as I was. I was glad to see it.

" You are really going to leave us on Wednesday next, Nellie ? " Bertie said, lighting a cigarette.

" Yes, Bertie ; we are here to say good-bye," I answered, a tear starting to my eye.

" How long do you mean to be away ? "

" Perhaps I may never come back. I must follow my mother's fortunes."

" Don't say that, Nellie. You will pay us a visit now and then ? "

" I should like it much, but the journey is long. I should be afraid of taking it quite alone."

" I might come and fetch you."

" Oh, that would make all the difference !
But you would be too busy, and you may
forget your little friend."

" Never ! " he shouted, getting up from
his seat, and throwing his cigarette away.
" It is far more likely that the gay life of
a continental city will drown the recollec-
tion of your dull life here."

" Dull, do you call it ! It may seem
dull to you, coming from gay Paris and
bustling London.   I wish for nothing
brighter or happier than the life I have
spent in the forest—at least, when you
were at home."

" You will change your opinion, Nellie,
and, besides—— "

" Besides what ? "

" Your mother is a foreigner, and will
follow foreign ways."

" What are you driving at, Bertie ? "

" She will arrange a marriage for you.
They all do, without consulting their
daughters.   Your husband will be an

Italian, with a black beard and a blacker heart. I hate Italians! they are all brigands!" and Bertie stamped his foot.

"I shall never marry any one but an Englishman," I said very quietly.

"Will you swear to that?"

"I will swear that no foreigner shall ever be my husband. There's my hand on it."

"Oh, Nellie!" he cried, holding my hand as if he would never let it go, " don't leave me!"

"I must, Bertie. You know I must go with my mother."

"Is there no way of keeping you in England?"

"None whatever. We start next Wednesday."

"If you married an Englishman, you would have to stay."

"But I am not going to marry an Englishman. I am not going to be married any more than you are, Bertie."

"How do you know that I am not going
to take to myself a wife? There is some-
body I would marry to-morrow, if I
could."

"Some fine London lady, I suppose."

"I have not spoken to a woman in town,
except our landlady and the slavey."

"A Paris demoiselle, then?"

"Catch me marrying a French girl!"

"Who can the lady be?" I asked, with
a flutter at my heart and a sparkle in my
eye.

"She is young and beautiful, sweet and
fresh as a May morning. She sings like a
nightingale. There is not in the wide
world another girl so pure and good."

"Dear me! What a piece of perfection
she must be! I should like to know her.
Where does she live?"

"In the New Forest."

"In the New Forest! Who can she
be? Have you asked her to marry
you?"

"I dare not. She is high-born, and an heiress; and she does not love me—not at least, as I love her."

"Poor Bertie! How can you tell, if you have not spoken to her?"

"I am afraid to speak. She might think I loved her for her position, her money."

"Faint heart never won fair lady. Ask her, Bertie. I wish I could help you. Have I ever seen this lovely girl?"

Bertie still held my hand, and I did not try to take it away. He pulled me up gently from my throne, and led me down to the stream, where it lay sleeping in a quiet pool.

"Look there!" he said. "You will see the girl I love."

I saw the reflection of my own face, and Bertie's looking over my shoulder.

"Not me, Bertie?" I cried. "You don't love me?"

"Who else but you?"

"I am no heiress; I am a poor girl. High-born! Why, I cannot even claim my father's name. I am worse than nobody."

"Is it true, Nellie? That would be too delightful!"

"Delightful that I should be fortuneless and nameless?"

"Yes, Nellie; because I might then dare to love you."

"You could love me, Bertie—poor, an outcast!"

"I have loved you from the day I drove you first from Lyndhurst Road Station. I love you with every bit of love in my heart, and shall love you till I die."

"Oh, Bertie, I can't believe it! It is too good to be true."

"Then, you love me, Nellie, you dear, sweet darling! My own, my very own;" and he led me to my throne, and, sitting down beside me, wrapt me in his arms, and kissed my breath away.

"I love you as you love me. I think I should have died, Bertie, if you had let me go without a word."

"Without a word! As if I should have let you go, my love, my life! It is not like saying good-bye now, is it, darling? Our parting is only the commencement of our union."

"It is only a sweet *au revoir*. You will come and see me soon at Florence, won't you, Bertie?"

"If I can spare the money and the time. I must work away and save, that I may make haste and build a nest for my bonnie bird."

"I must help to find a few twigs, too."

"You must leave nest-building to me, darling. What could you do in the way of money-making?"

"As much as you, perhaps, Bertie; that is, if you will let me."

"I certainly shall have no objection to your turning an honest penny."

"Penny, indeed! I shall go in for guineas—hundreds of guineas."

"Where is your gold mine, darling?"

"In my throat. Mother says my voice is splendid, and that if I go on the stage I shall make a fortune."

"I should not like that, Nellie. I would rather see you poor than rich by singing at the opera."

"That is English prejudice! In Italy, I should be a queen. Look at my mother! She is good and noble, and a prima donna."

"And would not my timid little Nellie be frightened to sing before a crowded theatre?"

"Not a bit. I forget everything when I am singing. I see nothing, and hear only my own voice. I shall be able to sing with so much more feeling and sentiment now that I know you love me. I shall always sing to you. You must come and hear me, Bertie."

"I could not bear to see another man making love to you, even in a play."

"You need not mind that. My mother says that it is all jealousy and hatred between actors and actresses. There is no love-making behind the curtain. You will let me try my luck, won't you, dear love?"

"I must have a talk with the signora; her experience is most valuable."

"No, Bertie, you must not speak to my mother. We must keep our engagement to ourselves for the present. Both the mammas will be against us, and talk prudence. I know what prudence means —to me, at least. It means a broken heart. We are young, Bertie, almost boy and girl. Let us keep our secret for the present, and in the meantime we can set about collecting materials for our nest. You can trust me, dearest?"

"I can trust you as I trust in God. But the signora will see your engagement ring."

" You must not give me a ring, Bertie."

" I can't let you leave England without a ring to remind you of the giver."

" I am wearing now your Mizpah ring ; let that be the sign of our betrothal."

" No, darling, that will not do. It must be a new ring, to recall this blessed day, and make you think often of your own true love, when you are far away."

" Nothing could make me think more often of you, dear Bertie; for you will never be out of my thoughts. Believe me, it is better that mamma should not know just at present that I have promised to be your wife. She has not seen you yet, and it might make difficulties between us. Remember, though I love her dearly, I have not known her long. Stay, Bertie! Have you a sixpence in your pocket ? "

" I think I am worth that amount. What do you want to do with it, Nellie ? "

" It will answer all the purposes of an

engagement ring. Don't you know the old custom ? "

" Here it is, Nellie. What are we to do with it ? "

" I swear on this silver sixpence to be true to my plighted troth for ever and for ever. Say it after me, Bertie."

" I swear on this silver sixpence to be true to my plighted troth for ever and for ever. Who is to have the coin, Nellie ? "

" Break it in two."

" That is easier said than done ! " cried Bertie, as he bent the sixpence with his powerful fingers. " It won't break."

" It *must !* It will be no *gage d'amour* unless we each keep a part."

" There it goes, Nellie. Which piece will you have ? "

" The smallest. It will just fit into my locket."

" I think you might give me your locket, and I will give you another when we meet in London."

I took the little locket from my neck, and, placing the piece of the broken sixpence inside, fastened it to Bertie's chain.

"Thank you, my own sweet darling," cried Bertie, kissing me tenderly. "I will never part with your dear gift."

"Now I am yours, love, for ever and for ever," I whispered.

"For ever and for ever," repeated Bertie, solemnly, and sealed our bond with another kiss.

Two young hearts were one, each filled with a great peace. Earth seemed to have blossomed into heaven, as we sat together under the sweeping beech boughs. We looked into each other's eyes, and saw a new light there, the light of trusting love. We did not care to speak, but the beating of our own hearts made music in our ears. We were dreaming the same sweet dream, dreamed first in Eden, sweeter and more consoling now that Paradise is lost.

Birds were singing in the branches; butterflies were dancing in the sunbeams; the air was palpitating with the wings of happy insects. All nature was offering up a universal psalm of praise. We were the only human souls in all that musical and murmurous throng, and our praises ought to have been the loudest, as our happiness was the greatest; for we knew that the love with which our hearts were brimming would live through life, and after death be perfected in heaven.

On earth there must be partings, and the hour came when Bertie had to unclasp the arms that held me tight, and leave me in our Summer Palace, for time and tide and train will wait for no man.

A sweet farewell, a long embrace, and my own true love was gone. I watched his retreating figure leading the pony till it was lost in the green labyrinth of the forest. I picked up my basket, and started in the opposite direction for my home, soon to be my home no longer.

My feet were so light that they hardly hurt the daisies. But my feet were not nearly so light as my heart!

CHAPTER VII.

WITH THE SWALLOWS.

THE parting with Mrs. Annesley was a
real sorrow to mother and daughter. Perhaps the mother felt it the most. Though
the acquaintance was short in days, she
had found a lifelong friend in her hostess,
but one she did not expect to see again
for many a year, if ever. I, on the contrary, hoped that Mrs. Annesley and I
should meet before very long, and that
when I did come back it would be as her
son's wife.

It was a greater trial for me to leave my
dear dog behind. Rannock was old, and
the infirmities of age were coming on him

fast. He could no longer chase the rabbits, or follow the wood-pigeons from tree to tree, and if he had ever been a poacher his poaching days were over. I could not expect to find him alive on my return. I should have liked to have taken him with me to Italy, but Job thought that the long journey would kill him, and he and my mother agreed that if he survived the journey he would be miserable on the third floor of a town house, after the free out-of-door life he had always led. It was decided that I must leave him in Job's care. Poor dear old Rannock, the friend that had never failed me, always loving, always true! It was very hard to say farewell, feeling that I should never see those honest eyes again, never hear the joyous bark that had greeted me every morning for fifteen long years.

Grown woman as I was, I threw myself on the grass by my dear dog's side, and, sobbing, clasped my arms round his shaggy

neck. I covered his old head with kisses,
whilst he looked into my face and whined
pitifully all the time. I am sure he knew
that he was about to lose his mistress.
Job said he was too old to care for anything but a quiet stretch in the sun, and
that he would not miss me long. I knew
better.

Next morning we were to be off early.
Rannock met me without his usual bark of
recognition. He wagged his tail feebly.
I gave him a last hug. He looked at me
wistfully, lovingly, closed his eyes, and fell
dead at my feet.

I was overwhelmed with sorrow. Rannock's death seemed to snap the last link
that bound me to the days of my early
childhood. Nannie was lying in a cold
northern grave. Sister Lucy, if not really
dead, was as good as dead to me. She had
gone with some other sisters on a mission
of mercy to nurse and teach nursing in
Indian zenanas, and I had not heard of or

from her since the breaking out of the
Mutiny. I dared not think of her fate.
And now Rannock was dead, my own dear,
faithful Rannock!

My mother dragged me weeping from
the body of my dog. I could not say
farewell, but I embraced Mrs. Annesley
tenderly, kissed Mrs. Nutburn, and shook
Job's honest hand warmly. My mother let
me weep quietly till we approached the
station, when she begged me to dry my
tears. Her maid, Teresa, met us there
with most of the luggage.

I pulled down my veil to hide my red
eyes, and, settling myself in a corner of
the railway carriage, began to think of
Bertie. The love that I had gained was
more than a compensation for the love
that I had lost, and Bertie's image for a
time drove Rannock's from my thoughts.
I could not meet Bertie with sorrow on
my face.

He was waiting on the platform at

Waterloo Station, and insisted not only on driving with us to Charing Cross, but on going down with us to Dover. I saw that he made at once a favourable impression on my mother, with whom he glided into intimacy without any effort on his part. He and I behaved, as I thought, most discreetly, though my mother must have been very blind if she did not see the love-light in our eyes, and notice the centrifugal force which drew us together, like two bubbles on a stream. I told him of Rannock's death, and the tears came to his eyes when I expressed my conviction that the dear dog had died of a broken heart at the thought of losing me.

We dined together at the Lord Warden Hotel, when Bertie found an opportunity of giving me a lovely locket, with A. E. I. in diamonds on one side. Though he anticipated one objection by telling me that his kind uncle, who was in his confidence, had supplied the purchase-money, he could not answer another. How was I to wear so costly an ornament without betraying our secret to my mother? I could only conceal it inside my dress. This was a disappointment to us both, but it was too late to rectify the mistake.

I could not speak for the lump in my throat, as we walked to the pier. When should I see Bertie again? Darkness was very kind to cover our parting on the steamer's deck.

My mother and I stayed a week in Paris, that my wardrobe might be replenished with clothes more suitable to my age and new home. Forest frocks were not quite the thing for fashionable Florence, and clump-nailed boots would have looked out of character in the Cascine Gardens.

We travelled in a *coupé lit* direct from Paris to Bologna, sleeping in our rumbling beds across the fertile plains of France to wake as the sun was peeping over the

Dent du Chat, and flooding the Lac de Bourget with rosy ripples.

On and up the panting engine drew us, passed Aix and Chambery, till the mountains closed their rugged arms around us, and, as we were looking up at their dazzling crowns, plunged us into the dark bowels of the earth, to shoot out on the other side of the Mont Cenis into light—and Italy!

Down we glided through the fastnesses of the hills into the sunny vale of Susa, and rattled on over the great Lombard Plains, smiling with olives, vines, and mulberry trees, past Turin on the rushing Po, and cities with liquid and well-known names, Piacenza, Parma, Modena, till the leaning towers of Bologna bowed to us as we approached our resting-place.

There we stayed a day to regain our breath, after our race with the wind, and my eyes learned to appreciate the warm beauty of Italian life. I could understand my mother's enthusiasm for the land of her birth, as I saw the deep shadows cast from the overhanging eaves in the narrow streets. I walked under twilight arcades in a mediæval dream, past palaces and churches warm with the glow of the South and the tints that only time can paint. Everything was a delight to my eyes—the careless life in the streets; the changeful groupings round the fountains; the open shops, where the potters and brassworkers were making vessels after models which were old in the days of the Carracci; the lumbering wains ; the strange trappings. of the horses. Everything I saw formed a picture full of glowing warmth and local colour.

My mother was delighted with the admiration I expressed, but promised me that I should find Florence even more beautiful and interesting than Bologna. I longed to cross the Apennines. They were but molehills to the Alps which we had passed, but they gave us more trouble to traverse them, as a huge block of granite had fallen across the rails near the summit of the pass, and we had to wait till another train could be telegraphed up from Florence. The southern slopes were blushing in the sunset as we slid down into the twilight plain where Arno winds and wanders. Dusk suddenly darkened into night. Pistoja and Prato were only names to tell us we were near our journey's end, and the lights of Florence were soon around us.

We were in Florence—Florence, my mother's home, and now mine, too. My mother lived in the Via Borgo Santi Apostoli, in the ancient palazzo of the Castracane family. It was not one of the grand old palaces of Florence, not such as the Palazzo Strozzi close by, in the Via Tornabuoni, or the Riccardi in the Via Cavour, where the rough-hewn blocks that form the walls of the *pian terreno* have the grand beauty of strength, and the whole edifice resembles more a fortress than a dwelling-house, as was indeed a necessity in the mediæval times when they were built. It was a large house, a wide expanse of white wall towards the street, with rows of green-shuttered windows, and overhanging eaves. Inside was a large quadrangle, round which the house was built, each story having its own open gallery. It seemed a long way to the top story, especially in the dark. I thought we should never reach the marchesa's apartment. Our delay on the mountain had made us several hours late, so that we were not expected. We found my great-grandmother and Signor Tagliano at a game of tresette, which I found was their amusement every evening of the year. Great was their joy at seeing my mother looking so well and so happy; and whilst they were embracing each other in true Italian style, I had plenty of time to take their portraits mentally.

The marchesa was a fine-looking old lady, with the remains of great beauty, her dark eyes still retaining much of their fire and animation. She was not so tall as her granddaughter, but probably she had shrunk a little from age. She was seventy-six, but did not look it. Her hair was snow-white, and drawn off her forehead in the style then called à *l'Imperatrice.*" A black lace scarf was thrown over her head, and tied under her chin. Her dress was of black satin, made in an old-fashioned style—opening in front, the right side folding over the left, leaving the neck uncovered. On her shoulders she wore an old lace shawl, crossed over her breast and tied in a loose knot behind. Her arms were bare below the elbow, finishing in the most lovely little hands sparkling with rings. The marchesa was a charming old lady to look at, *aristocrate jusqu aux bouts des doigts.*

The first violin was a little man, some

fifteen years her junior, neatly made,
though his feet and hands were too
large in proportion to his figure. His
features were rugged, with an aquiline
nose and overhanging brows. They
would have been considered plain, if they
had not beamed with intellect and good
humour.

Both the marchesa and Signor Tagliano
stared at me with mute astonishment. She
ran up to me and embraced me, kissing me
on both cheeks.

"Che, che! She is a woman!" she
cried, holding me at arm's length.

"A very beautiful woman," added the
first violin, coming forward and kissing
my hand.

"Did you expect to see a baby in a
cuscino, grannie?" asked my mother,
laughing.

"We expected a child, did not we,
Luigi?"

"Certainly, marchesa. Our Bice never

led us to think that her little Nella was a *donzella*."

"She is not like you, Beatrice mia," said the old lady.

"She is an English blonde," remarked the violinist; "but her eyes resemble her mother's."

"Her voice is Italian," said my mother; "very like mine in timbre. You think I have a fine organ, maestro?"

"Grand, divine."

"Wait till you hear Nella's. It is fuller, sweeter than mine ever was. Of course, it wants training."

"Does she mean to study?" asked Tagliano.

"Of course, I do. I want to go on the stage," I answered.

"Evviva!" cried the marchesa. "She will make a *furore* with her golden hair."

"If they think more of my hair than my voice, I must cut it off. I want my voice to be first."

" Nella is only joking in talking of
becoming an opera-singer," put in my
mother. " I wish her to study; but the
stage—no!"

" Why not, mother dear ? "

" One in the family on the stage is quite
enough."

" Are you jealous, Beatrice mia ? " asked
my great-grandmother.

" Jealous of my child! I know she
will be a finer singer than I have ever
been, and the more she surpasses me, the
prouder shall I be. But I do not wish
her to go on the stage. It is a very
trying life; and, besides, her father might
object."

" I have no father! He has discarded
me!" I cried. " I have only you to think
of. If you will not allow me to appear
before the footlights, I shall obey you;
but I should like to make money. What
is the use of hiding my candle under a
bushel ? "

"Let her try, Beatrice," said the violinist. "If her voice is as fine as you say, it would be a sin not to allow it to be heard."

"What does grandmamma say?" my mother asked.

"You have not been as strong as you used to be. You want rest. It is better to give up singing before it gives you up. Nella might take your place."

"I know my voice is not what it was; but I want to make a better provision for my daughter, now that she is cast off by her father and his people."

"The child could provide for herself!" cried Tagliano. "She would make a fortune, as you would have done long ago, if you had not had scruples which led you to refuse engagements in Paris and London. She will be able to take the money of those ignorant people, and then come back to sing to us, who know what music is."

" I should never care to go on the stage, mother, if you left it. I want to sing with you."

" That could never be, dear child. We Italians are funny people, and a mother and daughter on the stage at the same time would not be tolerated. I should be thought too old, and should be told so in very plain language."

" Then I will never go on the stage, if I am to drive you off."

" You would be doing your mother a very kind turn!" exclaimed the marchesa. " The doctors have told her that she must give up singing before long."

" Well," said my mother, " as you are all against me, we will think it over. We'll see what Babbo and I can make of her. She learns fast; but she will want another year's study, at least, and for that time, at all events, I shall remain—— "

" The finest singer in Italy," interrupted Tagliano.

" And the most beautiful woman in Europe," added the marchesa.

" And the sweetest mother in all the world," I finished, with a loving kiss.

CHAPTER VIII.

FLORENCE.

How I revelled in the delights of Florence! Nature and art have fixed on the City of Flowers as the spot they both love to honour. I was never weary of roaming about the streets, finding new beauties everywhere; and as for the views from Bello Sguardo, San Miniato, and Fiesole, they almost made me think slightingly of the New Forest.

Our street, the Via Borgo Santi Apostoli, led into the Via Tornabuoni, the fashionable shopping street of Florence. At first I liked to look at the tempting wares in the windows, and the handsome equipages

filled with smart ladies, who seemed to
enjoy being ogled by the dandies on the
steps of the Café Doney; but my artistic
yearnings soon drew me off into less fre-
quented thoroughfares. The lanes round
Mercato Vecchio, the old market, were
favourite hunting-grounds for the pictu-
resque, and I put up with unsavoury
smells and unpleasant sights to regale my
eyes on scenes full of southern life and
mediæval memories. My mother, whose
æsthetic tastes were not so developed as
my own, refused to accompany me as often
as I wished into this delightful, but un-
cleanly, labyrinth; and deputed her maid,
Teresa, to escort me in my researches after
cinque-cento dirt, as she chose to call it.

In more open and less unsavoury places
she delighted to be my companion. She
took me down the sunny, Lung' Arno to
the Cascine Gardens, by the river-side; to
the Ponte Vecchio, Florence's Rialto, where
the jewellers' little shops clung like limpets

to the old stonework of the bridge; to the
Piazza del Signoria, with its grand old
palace and tall belfry-tower, where Michael
Angelo's gigantic statue of David stands
on guard. I loved to sit on the edge of
the Triton's fountain, or on the steps of
the Loggia di Lanzi, and dream myself
back to the days when the piazza was the
mustering-place of the citizens called to
arms by the tocsin of the cow-bell; or
when it was crowded by the friends and
foes of Savonarola, to see him go through
the ordeal of the fire. She took me to the
Cathedral of our Lady of the Flowers, and
bade me admire Brunelleschi's dome and
Giotto's campanile. She made me sit on
Dante's seat, and then showed me the
bronze doors of the baptistery, which the
great poet said were worthy to be the gates
of paradise. She asked me what I thought
of Donatello's statue of our English St.
George outside the church of Or San
Michele, which is said to have been the

cause of the sculptor's death. His old
master told his pupil that it only wanted
one thing to make it perfect, but refused
to say what that one thing was. Donatello,
silly fellow, fretted himself into a fever,
and when the master was sent for and
told him all it lacked was life, he died
with a smile upon his face at such high
praise. My mother led me from church to
church—Santa Annunziata, with Ghirlan-
dajo's mosaic over the centre portal; San
Marco, where Savonarola preached and
prayed, and Fra Bartolomeo painted; San
Lorenzo, with the world-famed monuments of the Medicis, by Michael Angelo;
and many others—till my brain was an
architectural chaos, and I begged to rest
it in the Boboli Gardens, and feast my
eyes with peeps of Florence through the
cypresses, or on the heights of San Miniato,
where they could roam over the city at
our feet, and the rich plain of Arno, to
the blue mountains of Carrara on the far-

away horizon. We spent hours in the galleries of the Uffizi and Pitti Palaces. After weary hours of practising—for I never allowed my artistic wanderings in Florence to interfere with the training of my voice—I used to find strange revivifying powers in the works of the old masters. There is a sympathetic chord between the sister arts of music and painting in the hearts of those who practise either; at least, I found it so. An hour in the Tribune was a mental tonic which never lost its virtue. Where in the wide world is such a treasure-house? To decorate the walls of that one small chamber, Raphael, Correggio, Guido, Guercino, Titian, and Michael Angelo have contributed their *chefs d'œuvres.* It took me months to examine the pictures in the two galleries, and then I felt that I had hardly begun to discover their beauties. But if I linger over Florence and its art-treasures, my story will never come to an end.

I worked away at my singing with an earnest heart, and made such progress that Tagliano, who was my master, prophesied that I should be quite capable of making my *début* at the end of a year. I had the advantage of seeing my mother in several operas. She sung at the Pergola in " Ernani," " Rigoletto," "Gemma di Vergi," " Mose in Egitto," and " Lucrezia Borgia." I accompanied her to Genoa, where she performed at the Carlo Felice Theatre in " Maria de Rohan " and " Lucia di Lammermoor ; " and then to Venice, where she sung in the operas of " La Forza del Destin " and " Petrella's Mario Visconti " at the Fenice. In all she sung and acted superbly, and was received with thunders of applause, her benefit nights being as lucrative as enthusiastic. I never knew in which part I liked my mother best. Her interpretations of each character were as natural as they were artistic. At one time I thought I preferred her Lucrezia, at another her Lucia, and then again she seemed to me to eclipse herself in the highly tragic part of Leonora, in "La Forza del Destin," an opera which has never been properly appreciated in England.

But I could not fail to remark her growing exhaustion when the performances were over, and to feel that she was exerting herself beyond her strength. This made me study with redoubled energy, as I knew that nothing would make her give up singing, except my *début*, and that if I was not successful she would continue on the stage. I must hurry my *début*, and secure a success. Her grandmother and Tagliano implored her to spare herself more, and not to throw herself so passionately into the parts she played; but she insisted that her dear public should have all her powers as long as they lasted. They both saw that the only chance of saving my dear mother from a thorough breakdown of strength depended on me, and they did all in their power to help and encourage me in my exertions. The first violin brought a declamation master from Milan, and obtained permission for me to take my lessons on the stage of the Pergola. It was hard work, but filial love gave me power to conquer difficulties, which at first appeared insurmountable, whilst Bertie's dear letters gave me heart for fresh exertions.

At the end of the year both masters pronounced me fit to make my appearance on the stage, with the certainty of success. I felt that I could do so without fear of failure, but was not so confident of making any great sensation. I knew that, as the daughter of the most popular prima donna in Italy, I should be sure of a *succés d'estime;* but the very fact that I was her daughter would naturally lead to comparisons, which could only be in her favour, and, therefore, against myself. But I determined to do

my very best. My success must be gained
by my own powers, or it would not be a
success at all.

It was not difficult for my mother's
daughter to procure an engagement, and I
had many offers. My mother and Tagliano
fixed upon Piacenza as the theatre for my
début, and "La Sonnambula" as the opera.
It was the same opera in which my mother
had made her first appearance in Florence,
and they thought it was a part not only
sympathetic, but suited to my girlish looks.

The marchesa told me I need not be
nervous, as my long golden hair in the
sleep-walking scene would bring down the
house. I could not help laughing at
the difference between the dear old lady's
idea of a success and mine. I did not
think much of a *succés de chevelure*. I
let her amuse herself with arranging my
dresses, as I knew her taste was perfect;
but the "Sonnambula" is not an opera
which requires much of the costumier.

All the members of the little family on the top floor of the palazzo were looking forward with great expectation and interest to the opening of the theatre at Piacenza. I believe at that time the least nervous of the party was the most concerned in the coming ordeal, and that was the *debutante* herself.

CHAPTER IX.

"LA SONNAMBULA."

THE operatic season at Piacenza, like that at most theatres in Italy, was to commence on San Stefano's day—the day after Christmas; but I had to be in Piacenza on the 12th of December, for rehearsals. In Italy, where music is in the people's soul, an imperfectly rehearsed opera would not be tolerated, as it is in unmusical England, where performances are applauded which would be hissed off the stage in the smallest theatre in Italy.

My mother, Tagliano, and Teresa accompanied me. The marchesa, though she never left Florence except in the height of summer, was so excited at the *début* of my golden hair that she would have come with us, but the weather was so bitter that her doctor forbid her to think of leaving the house.

Nothing was to be spared in the way of expense to give *éclat* to my first appearance on the stage. The best apartments were engaged at the best hotel, and a carriage and pair met us at the station. My mother's name and occupation secured us a warm reception. All the members of the *Direzione*, which generally consists of the mayor and half a dozen of the leading inhabitants of the town, paid their respects at once, and made much of me for my mother's sake. They wished me a tremendous success. Tagliano assured them that their wishes would be fulfilled, as, with a little experience, I should take a very high place amongst dramatic soprani.

The day after our arrival, rehearsals commenced as usual in the apartment of the soprano, only the leading artistes taking part in it. The *direttore d'orchestra* was at the piano, and the mayor and three of the *Direzione* were present—a special compliment, as they seldom appear before the orchestral rehearsals at the theatre. We saw at once that the tenor was quite unequal to the part, and, though I felt for the poor young man, I was not sorry to find next day that he had been dismissed, and another tenor secured by telegram from Milan. He also was a failure, and another was telegraphed for.

At last the principal characters in the opera were creditably filled, and we set to work in earnest to secure a good *ensemble*. A week before the opening of the theatre, the rehearsals were transferred to the stage, when orchestra and chorus were in attendance. We sang through our parts without books, seated in position, and very comical was the effect, when Elvino and myself, on two chairs, sang a love duet, doing all the business from the waist upwards, but sparing our legs all unnecessary fatigue. At first it was impossible to control my risible muscles, as the tenor looked unutterable things, expressing the emotions of his heart with eyes and hands only; but when I saw how serious all the others were, I learned that it was no laughing business. The chorus, chiefly inhabitants of the town, recruited by some leading voices from Milan, walked about, or lolled against the scenery, whilst the concerted music was being gone through with full orchestral accompaniments. I began to feel that the part of a prima donna was not only very fatiguing, but most unpoetical. Before and behind the curtain are very different worlds.

At last came the *prova generale*—a day of great importance to the singers. The theatre was partially lighted, and all the members of the *Direzione*, with their families, and the subscribers to stalls and

boxes have the privilege of being present.
The chorus appear in costume; the principal characters in evening dress. My
mother was most careful that my dress
should be becoming, as the prima donna
who wins approbation and appplause at the
prova generale has a large body of sup-
porters at the first public representation.
She is not expected to exert herself
through the whole of her part, as it is
important that she should be spared fatigue,
and save her voice for the opening night;
but it is the practice to give one scene
with all the feeling and power of voice
and action at the singer's command. I
reserved myself for the final scene, which
I gave to the best of my ability, encouraged
by occasional "bravas" from the side-
scenes, where my mother, Tagliano, and
some members of the *Direzione* were standing. At the conclusion I was greeted with
a shout of genuine applause from the half-
filled theatre. The unusual noise, coming

out of the dimly lighted house, quite frightened me, and I stood staring, like one in a dream, at the audience.

"Avanti, e salutate il publico!" cried my mother. Her sweet voice brought me back to my senses, and I made the most graceful obeisance of which I was mistress.

I returned to the hotel very pleased with the result of the *prova*, the orchestra having joined in the applause, which is only customary in cases of very special excellence. My mother and the first violin were delighted at my reception, and promised me a *furore* on the opening night. They implored me not to look frightened at the applause, as I had done, but to keep a stock of smiles in store, and to be ready with the most graceful of the curtsies I had practised before my looking-glass.

Next day, being Christmas Day, was *riposo*. I much needed a day's rest after the fortnight's hard work. I had seen little of the town, except in my drives to and from the theatre. It seemed to me that Piacenza was a misnomer. It was anything but a *plaisance* in my eyes; only a dull, dreary town. The principal piazza, with its two equestrian statues of Farnese dukes, had no bright Italian life in it. Piacenza had no living heart, for in all Italian towns the piazza is the heart to which all the life of the community flows. I found, however, later that Piacenza had a heart for music, and a very warm heart, too.

The evening of the 26th arrived. The ordeal of my life was at hand. I had not felt the least nervous before. Now I should have liked to have taken the next train and travelled from Piacenza, Italy itself, and hidden my head in the depth of the New Forest. I knew I was note-perfect in my part; but could I bring the notes out when I saw the theatre filled with rows of white faces? My mother and Tagliano laughed at my fears, and asked why I had been so courageous at the *prova generale.* I could not explain the reason, except on the score of health; for never before had I been nervous in singing, or expected to feel nervous. I saw that my mother, spite of her endeavours to laugh me out of my fright, was pale with nervousness herself, and Tagliano's big nose was red from the same cause. He kept on blowing it for occupation, and paced the room like a lion in a cage.

It was a great relief when the carriage was announced. It was a cold night, and I hugged myself in my furs. I closed my eyes, and would gladly never have opened them again. The theatre was a blaze of light, and crowds were waiting *en queu* at the entrances to the pit and galleries. I stepped out at the stage door like one in a dream, and walked mechanically to my dressing-room, through rows of bowing carpenters and choristers. My little dressing-room, like those in most Italian theatres,

was on the stage in the *coulisses*. I could
see from the door all that was going on
on the stage, and required no prompter's
boy to call me. I dressed quietly for my
part, with my mother's and Teresa's help.
They talked to each other of all sorts of
theatrical experiences, when my mother
had sung the part of Amina. They purposely left me in peace when my dressing
was finished. They told me my costume
was most becoming. I did not care how
I looked. The *Direzione* were all behind
the scenes, and I heard the mayor tell my
mother that he had never seen such a
brilliant house in Piacenza, that my success
at the *prova generale* had set the whole
town on the tiptoe of expectation. Was it
of me they were talking? I heard the
tuning up of the orchestra, and then the
overture began. My heart seemed to come
up into my throat at the last bars. The
curtain drew up; there was a buzz through
the house, and then silence. Teresa came

towards me to be ready to take my fur cloak. The stage became crowded with peasants singing, "Viva Amina!" and I was Amina! My head went round at the bare thought. Lisa's "Cavatina" followed, and, after the duet between her and her lover, Alessio, the chorus went on again with "Viva Amina!"

Teresa seized my cloak, and almost tore it off my shoulders. My mother gave me a fond kiss and a pat of encouragement upon my shoulder. I was still dreaming. "Coraggio, avanti!" she cried, and pushed me forward. I found myself in the centre of the stage. I looked up, and saw the theatre crowded with row upon row of up-turned faces. I did not know who I was or where I was. I stood petrified with a strange sort of fear. The orchestra stopped for a moment, and the clapping of many hands woke me from my dream.

"Salutate," I heard some one whisper from the flies. I bowed mechanically, and

I think my face wore anything but a smile. The orchestra struck a chord or two. "Coraggio!" came from the prompter's box; "Comminciate."

I heard a sweet clear voice singing "Care Compagne." The chorus of girls flocked round me. The voice went on, giving the notes with perfect accuracy and with much feeling, and then broke into the andante, "Come per me sereno." "Brava, brava!" came from the coulisses. That was mother's voice; and now Tagliano's. I heard a "brava" here and there in the house, and then, after an elaborate cadenza, the voice stopped, and the air rang with a storm of bravas, accompanied by the clapping of a thousand hands.

It was my voice. I was Amina. I had sung well, or there would have been no applause. I must have sung very well for such applause as that! "C'est le premier pas qui coute," and I was over it. I was myself again, and in perfect possession of

my nerve. Every atom of fear was gone.
I felt as bold as I had felt the reverse.
I stepped forward and curtsied to the
ground, my face wreathed in smiles. The
applause grew louder. I placed my hand
on my heart and smiled my thanks. I
took my theatrical mother's hand again,
which I had dropped, and broke into the
brilliant allegro, "Sovra il sen," expressing
the love-rapture of my heart. I was
Amina, waiting the arrival of my lover,
Elvino. I sang as I had never sang before,
as I never thought I could have sung.
The notes came out sweet and round and
full. I felt that I was pouring out the
love of my heart, not for the stage Elvino,
but for Bertie. I sang to him, of him, for
him, and him alone. My eyes glistened
with love, my heart was beating with love,
and my voice was full of love. The song
was over. Oh, the roar that greeted me!
It was very pleasant to my ears, but rather
louder than I cared for. I approached

quite close to the footlights, and curtsied low. I smiled as my eyes wandered round the house, and from the pit to the highest gallery. I gave them all my smiles—not the smiles of affectation, but of supreme happiness. I had saved my mother's life, I was on the road to fortune, and my Bertie. I had made my *début*, and was more than satisfied. It was all plain sailing now. I had only to rest on my laurels till the end of the first act.

The curtain fell. I was in my mother's arms. She was weeping and laughing hysterically at my success. Oh, the joy of having fulfilled her expectations and those of my kind maestro, Tagliano! A hundred happy thoughts flashed through my brain, till they were banished by the roar of voices shouting " Nella Bardi." It did not strike me that it was my name till one of the *Direzione* came forward to offer me congratulations, and to lead me to the side of the curtain, where Elvino was waiting to conduct me across the stage. I curtsied time after time, no longer frightened by the noise, but delighted at its volume. I was recalled three times, and had to repeat my smiles and curtsies.

In the second act there was no special opportunity of displaying my vocal powers, but my audience evidently appreciated my *mezza voce* in the sleep-walking scene, and in the scene where Elvino is led to suspect me, and finally to cast me off. I sang with all the dramatic power I possessed. Real tears were in my eyes; there were tears, too, in my voice. I felt that I had touched the hearts of the audience, and the curtain fell upon a secured triumph. The *Direzione* came up one after the other, as I sat with one hand in my mother's, the other in Tagliano's, and congratulated me on a *succés fou.* " Nella Bardi! Nella Bardi ! " came through the curtain, and I had to appear again and smile my thanks. When I had crossed the stage three times, I began to think this part of the performance rather monotonous.

The greatest difficulty in the opera was still before me, but I had no fear of not getting over it with success. I was warm with the glow of victory, and felt confident of being victorious to the last.

The curtain drew up for the last act. The scene was received with a round of applause. It was a new decoration. The moon-lit mill was very realistic, and the whole picture was very charmingly painted. It was the work of a young scene-painter. An Italian audience, though it is always critical, and sometimes, perhaps, may appear cruelly severe, is always appreciative of good work, and has a kind thought for the humblest member of the *corps dramatique* who deserves encouragement. On this occasion they called for the painter of the scene, who so little expected to have such an honour paid him that he was in his painting blouse, and was hurried before the curtain in his coat of many colours, much to the amusement of the audience and his own distress.

I had practised walking the plank across the mill-wheel, and had no fear of a tumble as I stepped out of the mill with my lighted candle. I heard the plank fall behind me without a start, and sang the sweet sleep music with great simplicity and perfect composure, as I came down the stage. I knelt down, and gave the short pathetic prayer, "Gran Dio, non mirar il mio pianto," with real fervour. Then, rising slowly from my knees, I took Elvino's faded flowers from my bosom, and sang very softly and sweetly the dirge of all my hopes, as I let them fall through my fingers. The tears were in my eyes, and I was quite absorbed in the character I was playing. I was waked from my strange dream by the "Viva Amina!" of the chorus, and fell with a shriek of joy into Elvino's arms. That shriek had been my bugbear. I had practised it till I was weary, and was never satisfied with the result; now it came spontaneously from my heart. It was not acting, it was reality. It brought the house down, and the point which I feared the most became my greatest triumph. My unexpected success gave me fresh power, and I broke into the joyous "Ah Non giunge" with an *élan* that surprised me. It was the genuine outburst of a heart relieved of a great sorrow. I was proved innocent, and my lover was mine. We were united again, and our love would make

"Della terra un ciel d'amore."

If there had been applause before, it was a *furore* now. I was obliged to repeat the air. The curtain fell at last upon such a genuine success as even my mother had never won.

"I told you, Nella mia, that you would eclipse your mother," she said, as she embraced me over and over again; " but

I did not think it would be quite so soon."

"Any one could succeed in the 'Sonnambula,'" I said. "I shall never come near you in Lucia or Lucrezia. You must telegraph to great-grandmamma, and tell her that my hair has done it," I added, laughing.

I was torn from my mother's arms to go through a fresh series of curtsies before the curtain. My reception was more enthusiastic than ever, and it was many minutes before the audience, excited only as an Italian audience can be, suffered me to undress, and the lights to be turned out.

The papers were full of my wonderful success, and telegrams, containing warm congratulations, came to my mother by the dozen. I only had one, from Bertie, to whom I had telegraphed my triumph; but it was worth all the rest put together.

I sang for twelve nights in the same opera to crowded and enthusiastic houses, and my popularity culminated in an ovation on my benefit night, when I was literally buried in flowers and loaded with presents.

I came to Piacenza an unknown girl, and left it a prima donna, the talk of musical Italy. After all, it proved a real Piacenza to me !

CHAPTER X.

THE DUKE OF MALADETTA.

I WAS soon acknowleded as a queen of song. I sang in many theatres during the following year, and in several operas. My mother and Teresa always accompanied me wherever I went ; and the first violin was often of our party, as he took almost as much interest in my professional career as he had done in my mother's.

Everywhere I was flattered and *fêted*, and my Benefits were rich in receipts and ·presents. I found the life very fascinating. I was constantly on the move, seeing new places, and making new friends. I did not feel that the fatigue and excitement did

me any bodily harm, but I began to acknowledge to myself, and later to Bertie,
that the admiration which I met with on
all sides was feeding my vanity, and
creating an appetite for it, which was
anything but beneficial to my spiritual
growth. In my quiet moments I often
wished that I could give up the life I
was leading, and throw off the pleasant
slavery. But I could see that my marriage
was the only break I could look forward
to. Every night I sang was, I hoped,
bringing that happy day nearer, as it
added to the heap of twigs that were to
help in building our nest.

Bertie, from whom I had no secrets, was
as anxious as I was to hurry my retire-
ment from the stage. He told me that
he did not fear that I should be spoilt by
vanity, but he owned that he was inclined
to be jealous of my admirers, both off and
on the stage. I told him that he need
not waste a thought on my Elvinos and

Fernandos, as they cherished towards me no other feelings but envy, hatred, and all uncharitableness. They only wished to spoil my effects and make their own, and every round of applause I received made their part of lovers more difficult to sustain. Friendship, to say nothing of love, was impossible behind the curtain. Jealousy filled the heart of every performer—in which I dare say I should have shared had I any one to be jealous of.

I never had but one operatic friend—a buffo singer—and a dear kind friend he was. The line of buffo singers is so completely apart that they rest on their own merits, and have no rivalry to fear from the sentimental singers. They are the cleverest and most intelligent in every way. It requires education and real talent to be a buffo, and, consequently, there are very few on the operatic stage in comparison with tenors, baritones, and basses, whose name is legion. Poloni was a buffo

of the highest order. We became friends
the first night we played together. He
would criticize my acting, tell me what
I did best and what points I missed. He
would watch me with deep interest,
applaud me when I did well, reprove me
for a mistake. He was the cleverest actor
I ever met on the stage, and was as super-
excellent in tragedy as in comedy. He
could draw tears both of laughter and
sorrow. As Pappa Martini, in Cagnoni's
opera of the same name, he has often made
me weep. He used to invent new " business" for me, and I owed much of the
praise I received for my acting to his unselfish and intelligent instruction. When
he was acting in the same opera with me,
I felt I had a trusty friend by my side
to save me from all annoyances, and to
urge me on to higher excellence in my
art. I sang his praises so often to Bertie
that he said there was, at all events,
one singer of whom he might be jealous;

but I set his fears at rest by telling him that my friend had a dear little wife and baby daughter, who were the joy and pride of his heart. The happy love of that little family is one of the brightest memories of my short operatic career.

I was not, however, able to conceal from Bertie that I had been persecuted in more than one theatre by the attentions of members of the *Direzione*, the only gentlemen who have the privilege of an *entrée* behind the scenes. Now and again I came across one who forgot that an actress could be a lady, and that all beauty was not venal. I generally found that the highest born were the lowest behaved. I had, however, little difficulty in keeping these fine gentlemen in their places, and showing them that an actress, who respects herself, must be respected by others. Repulse in some cases only increased the attraction, and more than once I received honourable offers of marriage. There was one especially advantageous offer, which my mother would have wished me to acccept; but I had no love to give any one but my English painter. I would rather have lived on dry bread with him than be fed on dainties by any other husband. Bertie knew this well, and had the most implicit confidence in my love. I told him everything that happened to me, on and off the stage. I kept back nothing, wishing him to feel the perfect love and confidence that cast out fear.

But though I found I could rid myself of most of my admirers, there was one who stuck to me like a burr. I could not shake him off. He was a Neapolitan duke. I had seen him first when I was singing at the little summer theatre at Este, a *villaygiatura* of the Venetians. He had been introduced to me at the house of one of the *Direzione*, an eminent lawyer. From the moment he cast his dark, wicked eyes on me, I loathed him with a loathing which words fail to describe. I shuddered when he came near me, and at the same time felt a strange influence pass over me the moment he looked at me. He was singularly handsome, in the dark Italian style, well-bred, courteous in his manner, and a real lover of music, singing himself with skill and talent, which placed him above any amateur I had ever heard, and would indeed have given him by no means a second-rate position on the stage. He was a well-known *dilettante*, free with his money, as in his manners, when he was allowed to be. The Duke of Maladetta was as notorious for his libertinism as his liberality; and my mother, knowing his character, had warned me to avoid his society as much as was compatible with politeness, at the same time to be careful not to show him any marked antipathy, lest he should resent it. The duke was as vindictive as powerful, and utterly unscrupulous as to the manner he carried out his vengeance.

From the day we met he paid me
marked attention, and sickened me with
his compliments. To an Englishwoman,
Italian compliments are apt to sound exaggerated ; but the duke's compliments,
though always gracefully turned, seemed
to insult my common sense ; and yet I
dared not offend him by telling him that
I despised them and him. He sent me
every morning the rarest flowers. I should
like to have returned them, but my mother
would not allow me to do so. I never
wore his flowers, or allowed them to be
seen in our apartment. On my Benefit
night he threw me a huge bouquet, over
which hovered a diamond butterfly of
great value. I could not return it without
giving offence, as the presents given to a
popular *beneficiare* are considered honourable perquisites, to make up for the small
salaries of prima donnas in Italy. I had
to thank him for his gift, which was worse
still.

On leaving Este, I had an engagement
at Verona. When I came on the stage as
Lucia, I saw the black eyes of the duke in
the stalls. He again sent me daily flowers,
and was present at every representation at
the theatre. At my Benefit he flung me
another bouquet and another butterfly.
His attentions were very marked, but not
disrespectful. I received him with freezing
politeness. From Verona we went to
Turin, where I saw him the first night I
appeared at the Carignano Theatre in " La
Forza del Destin." There he sat, with the
everlasting *pince-nez* on his nose, well-
dressed, aristocratically handsome, and
devilish. He looked like a modern Mephistopheles. I shuddered when I felt his
opera-glasses turned upon me. His presence
in the theatre began to exercise a disturbing
influence on my acting, which my mother,
fortunately, was the only one to observe.
I *felt* his eyes. I could tell he was in the
theatre and the exact position of his seat

without seeing him. At first I thought it must be fancy, but night after night the conviction grew on me that there must be some mysterious mesmeric power which attracted me to look in his direction wherever he sat.

I could complain of no discourtesy. The duke had a perfect right to sit in the stalls, and any other actress would have thought herself honoured by being followed by such a good judge of music and so powerful a patron. His admiration was respectful and observant. I could take no exception to it. I was a public character, and must put up with admiration much less refined than his. I wished he would be rude or forward, to give me an excuse for refusing his flowers and his diamonds. I longed to pick a quarrel with the duke, that I might free myself from the growing slavery of his glance. As it was, I had to endure his hateful presence and the wicked glare of those hungry eyes.

We returned home, when he soon appeared at the Palazzo Castracane, and made desperate love to my great-grandmother, who thought him the most charming of men, and never ceased singing the praises of his handsome face and courtly manners. My mother often smiled at me as the old lady expatiated on his high rank and great possessions; but I only felt anger at the idea that the duke had bribed her by a course of bonbons, flowers, and a string of pearls (which was new, and his gift, I was convinced) to take his part. He paid us a daily visit, often in the evening, as the Pergola was closed, and condescended to play with the marchesa her favourite game of tresette. His eyes exercised on me a snakelike fascination, and made themselves felt, even when my back was turned, as I generally contrived that it should be.

I had signed an engagement to sing in three operas at the San Carlo, in Naples. I should not have accepted the engagement had I known that the duke had been instrumental in procuring it for me. When he heard, as it were for the first time, that we were going to Naples, he begged my mother to accept an apartment in one of his palaces. She found it difficult to refuse, especially as the duke's offer was backed up by her grandmother, who could not understand her declining it; but she did decline it, on the plea that she had already engaged an apartment on the Chiaja. She refused the duke's invitation as graciously as was compatible with refusing distinctly. The angry scowl and wicked flash in his eyes, transient but diabolical, did not escape me. The man began to inspire me with more than loathing, with abject terror. I felt it was quite in his power to paralyze my powers of singing and acting. He could ruin my theatrical career if he chose.

I was at my wit's end to know what course to pursue. My health was beginning

to suffer. My mother was afraid to interfere beyond speaking to my great-grandmother, who was very angry at my
refusing the honourable attentions of such
a rich and powerful nobleman. My mother
thought that if she spoke to the duke he
might turn upon her, and assure her that
she had entirely mistaken his admiration
for her daughter, that it was only the
admiration of a great lover of music for an
artiste of exceptional talent. My mother
thought he might say this. I did not.
But, at all events, she was afraid to broach
the subject. If it was indelicate for my
mother to interfere, it was impossible for
me. We did not like to take Tagliano into
our confidence, as he was hot-tempered,
and might have spoken to the duke in a
way which we might all have regretted.
My mother was almost as afraid of him as
I was, but she did not feel the mysterious
influence of his eyes—probably because he
did not exert it on her as he did on me.

The only means of coming to an understanding would be to induce the duke to open the subject himself. If my mother would not take the matter in hand, I must. I must try and bring on a declaration myself. The present state of affairs was simply intolerable. I had hitherto begged my mother never, under any pretext, to leave me alone with the duke. He had found, therefore, no opportunity of speaking to me in private. I would give him an opportunity. It is unusual in Italy for a young lady to be left to a *tête-à-tête* with a single man, but my professional position might be considered to have emancipated me from the etiquette of private life; now, at all events, I wished that I might find myself alone with my admirer, as if by chance. The difficulty was to get the marchesa out of the room, but my mother and I decided that it must be contrived in some way, and that we must so far take the first violin into our confidence.

I felt in better spirits that evening, and enjoyed my drive to the Cascine Gardens. It seemed that there was a prospect of throwing off the thraldom of those eyes, if I could bring the duke to declare his intentions. As soon as our carriage was drawn up near the band, I was conscious that the Duca di Maladetta was looking at me. I turned my head, and saw him exactly in the direction I expected. He came up to the carriage at once, and brought us sorbets and ices. They burned instead of cooling my throat, but I was afraid to refuse them. His voice was sweet, and his manners charming; but the eyes—the eyes were demoniacal. They fascinated me to that degree that I did not dare to encounter them, and always kept my own down when he addressed me. Those basilisk eyes were on my nerves. Was it weak health that had brought me to such a state that I could not stand their gaze? I was young, strong, and not given to attacks of nerves, like other girls. I was too hard-worked to be hysterical. There must have been a magnetic power in the eyes themselves to affect me so strangely, so painfully. Or why was the duke's presence, even when unseen, a torture?

I was to appear for the first time at Naples in a *rôle* new to me—that of Margarita, in "Faust." I felt that if the duke was in the house, I should break down; I should make a fiasco. It seemed very hard that the man who showed such admiration for me should bring me into such a trouble. I would appeal to his honour as a man and a gentleman to relieve me from the dread he caused me.

The next day fortune favoured us so far that the marchesa was confined to her bed with a chill, and Tagliano had gone to look at a vineyard he had bought above Pistoja. My mother and I were alone. I was practising my "Faust" music. A ring at the door announced a visitor. We called to Teresa, and instructed her, if it was the Duca di Maladetta, to return in the course of a few minutes, and say that the marchesa wished to see the signora.

It was the duke. Teresa played her part very spontaneously. My mother begged to be excused for a few minutes. I rose as if to follow her. The duke seized my hand to retain me. I shook it off, but stayed. My heart beat fast with nervousness and fear, but still I was glad to think that suspense would soon be over. I sat down on the chair from which I had risen, and picked up the embroidery I had dropped.

"Excuse the liberty I have taken, signorina," said the duke; "but I am anxious to have a few words with you alone, and fortune seemed inclined at last to give me an opportunity."

"An actress has to put up with much that a lady would not like," I answered.

"Have I ever treated you otherwise than as an equal in rank, signorina? To express a silent admiration is surely not disrespect!"

"I cannot say that you have, signor duca."

"Then, why is it that you always turn away from me?"

"Because you frighten me. Your eyes seem to pierce me through and through."

"I did not know they were so expressive; at all events, they can only speak their admiration. You must know, signorina, that I have only eyes for you; that I am your most devoted slave."

"Indeed, I wish that your eyes did not follow me; they make me shudder."

"Other women have not found them so alarming. Look at them, signorina! You will find they are ordinary eyes, but filled with admiration of your beauty. You have cruelly misjudged them. Look at them just this once!"

I did look at them, and, strange to say, without fear; the malign influence was not there. They were very beautiful eyes, with a wealth of tender love in their depths, which might have touched my heart if it had not been in Bertie's keeping. I could understand any woman returning the duke's love, if he looked at her as he looked at me.

"Are they very terrible?" he asked, with a voice of touching sweetness.

"I should not be frightened if they were always as they are now."

"They would always be the same to you. They could not help reflecting some of your beauty and goodness. You are the sweetest and loveliest woman they have ever looked upon."

"You are a flatterer, signor duca."

"I am speaking the plain, unvarnished truth. You have an attraction for me which no other woman has ever had—the attraction of virtue as well as beauty. I have struggled against the fascination which leads me after you from place to place, and will lead me wherever you go."

" Oh, don't follow me—don't!" I cried.

" You can spurn me, turn away from me, but you cannot keep me from your presence—in the theatre, at least. That is free to all who can pay for a ticket. I can admire you there, at all events."

" Yes, I know it, alas! too well. I am an actress, and public property, to be gazed at and annoyed by any one who has a lire in his pocket."

" Actress or not, you are the most beautiful woman in Italy, and the best."

" And you are high-born, handsome, a true musical genius, and yet you condescend to persecute a poor girl like me."

" Persecute you! Do you call it persecution to be admired by a man who has an historic title and a fortune to satisfy your every want—a man who only lives in your presence, and dreams of you when absent. Other women, I can tell you, would not call it persecution to be admired by the Duca di Maladetta."

"I am not like other women. I am a simple English girl, though I have Italian blood in my veins. I like to be admired and applauded, but not in your way."

"Not in my way! Oh, Nella, Nella! I love you as I have never loved before. Forgive me if I have frightened you, annoyed you by following you from theatre to theatre. I cannot help my love, and I love you, oh! my darling—love you with the passion of my life! I had sworn that no woman should ever enslave me; but you have conquered, where no one ever conquered before. Love me for my love. Try and love me, Nella mia."

"If you talk like this, duke, I must leave you."

"Why may I not talk to you in this way? My intentions are honourable. I know you too well, my darling—your pure white soul, your faithful heart—to dream of offering any but an honest love. I kneel at your feet, my Nella, and offer my name, my wealth; I, who have always hated the idea of marriage, implore you to be my wife, my duchess——"

"I thank you for the honour you have done me, signor duca, but it cannot be."

"You are only trying to make me more your slave. Don't play with my passion. I offer you rank and riches. Remember, it is no mean position to be Duchess of Maladetta. I offer you my love. That may not be worth much in your opinion, but it is the first true love I have offered womankind. I have been a bad man all these years, but it is in your power to make something out of me. The past shall be buried on our wedding-day, and you shall lead me to a better life—a life where love is pure and holy. Oh, Nella! I feel like a devil with just a chance of heaven; your love would bridge the gulf. There are tears in my eyes, my darling—tears of love

and repentance. I love you, Anima mia.
Do not thrust me back into the hell of
despair. I have loved you from the first
day I saw you, as you came down the
stage in your white dress and kissed the
faded flowers. You looked to me a saint,
an angel. A bad man knows what pure
eyes are, and I saw that your eyes were
wells of purity. Look at me, my darling!
Ah, your eyes are full of tears, too. Let
one drop on my cheek, and it will wash all
my wickedness away. Take me, Nella
mia! Make me worthy of your love. Be
my wife, my saviour wife!"

"It would indeed be a blessed task to
lead you to a better life," I said, deeply
touched by the duke's passionate pleading
for my love, "though I should be a poor
guide."

"A holy angel would not be a safer
guide!" he cried, seizing my hand.

I pulled my hand gently away. I felt
an intense pity for the man whose better

nature seemed to be struggling to conquer the evil to which he had been so long a slave. I saw that he loved me with a pure and purifying love, such as he had never known before. He no longer seemed repulsive in my sight. I looked upon his handsome face. The eyes were no longer terrible, but soft, with a world of love in their dark depths. And oh! how sweet was his voice, as it pleaded in the musical and melting accents of the Italian tongue! If I had not loved Bertie with a whole heart, I might have tried to love the duke and help to save him from himself. But it was too late. My love could never be his salvation.

"It cannot be, dear duke," I whispered sadly. "I cannot be your guide—not, at least, as your wife."

"You do not hate me now, Nella. The anger and fear has faded out of your face."

"No; I can look into your face without fear. Your good angel has taken all the wickedness out of your eyes. Keep your good angel. Never let him leave you again."

"You are my good angel. I want none other."

"I would sacrifice everything I possess, but one thing, to make you good and happy."

"What is that one thing?"

"Another man's love. I am pledged to be the wife of an Englishman."

"And you love him?" gasped the duke, turning livid.

"As my life. We have loved each other since we were children."

"Then, there is no hope for me?"

"None whatever."

"No hope, no hope!" muttered the duke, very piteously.

A struggle between good and evil seemed to be going on in his heart. For a moment I hoped that the good would carry the day, as he looked still lovingly at me. Suddenly the evil glare came back into his eyes. I shrunk before it, terrified, appalled.

"You refuse to be my duchess?" he shrieked, rising up before me like a demon, with arm outstretched as if to give me a death-blow. "You reject my love? Then, prepare to feel my hate. I have loved you as woman never was loved. You have made me your foe. Woe to the man or woman who has me for an enemy! None has ever escaped the vengeance of the Duke of Maladetta."

"Spare me! oh, spare me!" I cried, in an agony of terror.

"Spare you? Never! I will bring you grovelling to my feet. I, who fear neither God, nor man, nor devil, will make you cry to me for pity, and will laugh at your cries. You think yourself a fine lady with your false airs of modesty and virtue. Look to your virtue; it will not stand you in much stead against the influence of my eyes. You were right in saying that my

eyes are terrible. They are, for they can
mould you to my will. The devil gave
them me to work his ways. You think to
teach me manners, and bring me to the
level of your contemptible colourless existence! It is you who want to be taught
what life is, and I will teach you! It is
I who say it—I, Alberto Duca di Maladetta.
My eyes have ruined many, and they shall
ruin you."

I stood shaking like an aspen leaf.
Anger, sorrow, disgust, fear, and at the
same time a strange liking for the man
I loathed, were the mingled feelings that
agitated my breast.

"Spare me!" again I cried. "You said
you loved me; spare me for the love you
bear me. I would have tried to love you
had I not given all my love to another.
Go your way, and let me go mine. The
world is large enough for us both. Leave
me, friend and enemy; give me neither
love nor hate."

" That can never be," he answered more calmly. " I give you the choice: friend or foe ; love or hate. Choose! "

" Then you must be my enemy and give me hate."

" So be it. I may bring you to love me yet, but I must work your ruin first. When you are hissed off every stage, you will come to me for help, and perhaps for pity. My love will then repay you for lost fame, my wealth for a lost livelihood. You will cease to be an actress, but you will be a duchess."

He seized me in his arms and gave me one passionate kiss.

" My love, you shall love me yet," he cried.

" Mother! mother! " I shrieked.

" What is the matter ? " cried my mother, bursting into the room. " Has the duke insulted you, my child ? "

" I have insulted your daughter by asking her to be my wife. She has rejected my suit.   But, duchess or no duchess, she shall be mine some day ; " and the Duke of Maladetta bowed himself to the door. " I shall have the pleasure," he added, as he left the room, " of being present at your first appearance in " Faust " at the San Carlo, on the twenty-fifth.   I shall come back expressly from Paris.   It will be a treat I cannot miss."

I knew what he meant.

CHAPTER XI.

A FIASCO AT NAPLES.

I WANTED to give up my engagement at the San Carlo. My mother and the first violin were against me, and laughed at my foolish fancies, as they called them. They said that the duke's threat should brace my nerves to higher effort, and gain me a greater triumph. But they did not know his power; had never been under the influence of his eyes.

I felt that the part of Margarita, in Gounod's opera of "Faust," was specially suited to me. With my light hair, I should look the German maiden to the life. The music lay well within my voice, and showed off my best notes. It might have been written for me. There was greater scope for sustained power in acting the character than in any opera I had studied, or perhaps the character was more sympathetic to me than others. I knew that I was capable of great things, and could score a triumphant success, if my efforts were not rendered abortive by the man who loved and hated me at the same time. He knew his power over me, and intended to exercise it, I was convinced.

I had just one hope that he had made a mistake as to the day of my first appearance at the San Carlo. He had distinctly said that he would meet me at the theatre on the twenty-fifth. The twenty-third was the date fixed for the commencement of my engagement. I should be thankful to get through one representation without his malignant presence. It would save my professional character at Naples.

We left Florence three weeks before the

twenty-third, as the rehearsals would be heavy. I had three operas to rehearse, "Faust," "La Forza del Destin," and "Gemma di Vergi." Our apartment on the Chiaja commanded a glorious view of the bay of bays, where heaven seems to come down to kiss earth and sea, and all mingle in one sweet embrace. The beauty of nature had a soothing influence on mind and body, weary as they were with long rehearsals; and our evening drives along the shore, or in the environs of Naples, gave me strength to go through the fatigues of the following day.

My rehearsals promised well. I was overwhelmed with compliments from the *Direzione*, who told me that all Naples was raving about the beauty of the new prima donna, and only wanted to hear her voice to complete the charm. I tried to smile my thanks for all their pretty speeches, but there was always a black cloud in my sky.

The *prova generale* went off brilliantly. The house was half full, and the applause which greeted me in the garden scene, where I exerted all my powers, was tremendous. I was so accustomed now to applause that it did not move me as it used at first. I took it as my due, and, like the food I eat, I should have starved without it.

The twenty-third arrived. I passed the day in a dream. Neither my mother nor Tagliano alluded to the subject of my fear. To divert my thoughts, I proposed a drive in the afternoon ; and, though the day was still hot, enjoyed the view from the Villa Regina Isabella, looking down over vineyard terraces on Naples, glowing in the sunshine, and all the white towers from Portici to Sorrento, strung like pearls upon the emerald skirt of the fair sea-nymph Parthenope.

I was very nervous. My mother persuaded me to try some wonderful voice-improver. [

was sure it was a nerve-tonic, and swallowed
the mixture to please her, though I knew
that there was only one thing which would
calm my nerves—the absence of my lover-
enemy. I dressed quietly, and was ready
in my simple frock, my golden hair hanging down in two long plaits, before the
orchestra began to tune up. I looked
several times through the peep-holes in
the curtain. I saw a crowded house, but
no evil influence affected me. The duke
had not arrived, or I should have felt it.

I took my seat at the spinning-wheel,
ready for the *tableau vivant*, when Mephistopheles calls up the image of Margarita
to induce Faust to sign the contract. I
knew by the buzz of voices and the glare
from the footlights that I was being gazed
at by the whole house as well as Faust.
I could see nothing through the veil of
gauze used to soften the tableau. I sat
motionless, expecting to feel the malignant
influence of the duke's presence. I

breathed more freely; I did not feel it. If he had been in the remotest corner of the theatre, my heart would have contracted with a sickening fear. He was not in the house. He had mistaken the day, and was now probably just about to leave Paris. Words cannot describe the joyous relief to my mind. Not only was all my nervousness gone, but the change from fear to confidence had such an elevating effect that I knew I should sing and act as I had never done before.

I stepped quietly into the market-place with a composure that nothing could ruffle. A murmur of admiration ran through the house. My simple dress suited my fresh English style of beauty. I say it without any vanity. I felt I had the house with me. "Non sono bella ni damozella" fell from my lips in the dead silence of breathless expectation, like the notes of a silver bell. The hush was so complete that a pin might have been heard, if one had dropped. I was the simple, modest German maiden, sweet, guileless Margarita. I felt the shadow of my hapless fate upon me, and sang with touching pathos. A thunder of applause greeted me at the end of my first air. I was so absorbed in my part that I omitted to acknowledge it, and went on with fuller voice and deeper sentiment, as love for the first time crept into my maiden heart. The curtain fell on such a scene of excitement as I had not seen before. In critical Naples I was received as few prima donnas can hope to be received. I was called and recalled till I wished my audience were a little less enthusiastic.

In the garden scene the Jewel Song was rapturously encored. Ovation followed ovation. I had, however, reserved myself for the grand prayer in the last act. I began softly, increasing the volume of voice with each change of key, till I threw it out with all its power in the

triumphant notes of the major. I electrified myself. I electrified the house. The
audience rose *en masse*, shouting and
waving their handkerchiefs. I bowed and
smiled, and disappeared, to be recalled
again and again. The lights were out at
last, and the house was emptied; but my
triumph was not over. The horses had
been taken out of my carriage, and I was
drawn through the moonlit streets to my
apartments on the Chiaja by crowds of
enthusiastic admirers; and even then they
would not leave me in peace. I had to
appear on the balcony, and " Buona notte,
cari amici ; sono multo fatigata," at last
sent the shouting throng away, and left me
to recruit exhausted nature with supper and
sleep. I had scored an unparalleled success !

I repeated the part on the twenty-fourth.
There was no evil influence to hinder
another success as great as the previous
night. I was acknowledged by all the
journals to be the finest dramatic soprano

who had appeared on the stage of the San Carlo for many years. It was now too late for the Duke of Maladetta to ruin me professionally at Naples. Nothing could reverse the verdict after two such performances.

I went to the theatre on the twenty-fifth in fear and trembling. I tried to keep up a brave heart, and to brace my nerves against failure by thinking of the triumphant successes of the two last nights. The moment, however, that the scene opened, and disclosed me at the spinning-wheel, I knew that my enemy was in the house. A cold shudder went through me. The scene closed again, and I recovered. It was clear to me that the influence, magnetic or otherwise, was in the eyes themselves, and could only be exerted visually. The smallest covering between them and the object to be influenced acted as a non-conductor. It was a strange psychological experience, but I had ex-

perienced it so often that I was convinced
it was not imaginary. I knew that I
should feel it the moment I appeared in
the market-place. I walked a few steps
without feeling the influence, but as soon
as I was in view of the stalls I was
suddenly stricken with the same chill; and
it seemed to me as if an unheard voice
said, "You shall not sing; you cannot
sing." I looked up, and met the wicked
black eyes. A will stronger than mine
was controlling me. I heard the orchestra
playing the bars previous to those to which
I was to sing my first notes. I tried to open
my mouth; my voice was gone. I gazed
imploringly in the direction of the cruel
eyes, which had a triumphant glare in
them, and not a grain of pity or regret.
I saw it was hopeless to conciliate them.
I gave one wild glance round the house,
pressed my hands to my forehead, and fell
prostrate on the hard boards. The curtain
came down. The influence was inter-

rupted. I was myself again, only bruised by the fall. Three doctors were on the stage in a minute, who felt my pulse and offered restoratives, as I lay in my mother's arms. They were puzzled, as they could not find a cause for my sudden seizure, nor for my as sudden recovery. The doctor's urged me to go on with my part, but I declined positively to appear again. I was so prepared for a breakdown that I had privately arranged with a young soprano to be dressed and ready to take up my part. My misfortune was her fortune; for she pleased the house, and became later a favourite prima donna.

I left the theatre with my mother and Teresa. Next day I was visited by several members of the *Direzione*, who came to inquire after my health, and, on finding me quite recovered, pressed me to resume my character of Margarita that night. I told them the true state of the case, that the Duke di Maladetta had exercised some magnetic influence over me to prevent my singing, and that, unless he was excluded from the theatre, it was useless for me to make another attempt. They did their best to persuade me that it was a fancy that I ought to conquer, but told me at the same time that they could not keep a subscriber from his seat. This being the case, I expressed my deep regret at breaking my engagement, and paid the forfeit money.

The duke had kept his word. He had driven me from the stage of the San Carlo, but he had not destroyed my reputation as a singer. I could accept no more engagements as long as he was alive and able to follow me from theatre to theatre. He had triumphed over the opera-singer, not over the woman. He had forced me to break my engagement with the *Direzione* of the San Carlo; he was powerless, thank God, to make me break my engagement to my *fiancé*.

l was crushed, professionally, for a time, at least. It was a severe blow to be obliged to retire from a calling in which I delighted, and which was bringing me to fame and fortune. I had one consolation that, though my purse and pride might suffer, nothing could take away the love and music in my heart.

My one great object was to get away from the neighbourhood of the duke. I could not breathe in the same air, so great was my indignation and disgust at his cowardly conduct to a woman. I must leave Naples at once, and without his knowledge. I could not return home, as naturally the first place he would seek me would be Florence.

It was very mortifying to have to leave Bella Napoli without visiting the places of beauty and interest in the neighbourhood, which I had hoped to have seen as soon as my engagement was over. I could not explore Herculaneum and Pompei. I could not ascend Vesuvius, or cross the blue sea to Ischia and Capri. I must give up the pleasure of a week or two of well-earned idleness, and all because one wicked man chose to punish me for not accepting the love he offered. But what was this loss, when compared to the loss of position on the stage which I had gained after so many months of hard work, to say nothing of the loss of income, which was to have helped me to marry the man I loved, and to have provided me a home in dear old England?

Where was I to fly from this hateful man? My mother telegraphed for her adopted father the very evening of my discomfiture. He came at once, and would gladly have sought an interview with the duke. This I would not hear of, as no good could have come of it. All I wanted was to leave Naples secretly, that the duke might not follow me. Tagliano wisely suggested that we should depart by sea, and as a

steamer was starting that very night for
Marseilles, touching at Leghorn and
Genoa, he proposed that we should take
advantage of it. It was settled at once
that we should slip off in the darkness,
that my mother and Teresa should dis-
embark at Leghorn and proceed to Florence,
and that he and I should go on to Genoa,
and there take the railway for Como. We
would look out for a secluded villa, when
the whole party, including the marchesa,
would unite and spend a quiet summer on
the shores of the most beautiful of the
Italian lakes. My mother thought it a
delightful plan, and felt sure that rest in
such a lovely neighbourhood would restore
me to health and spirits, and enable me to
continue my operatic career.

I could see they all laughed at my
magnetic theory. It was a case of nerves
—nerves, and nothing more!

I wish it had been so!

CHAPTER XII.

THE soft beauty of the Lake of Como acted like a charm on my troubled spirits. The breezes brought the scent of flowers from the gardens which lined the shores, and healing on their wings. Towering mountains capped with everlasting snow, undulating hills green with chestnut trees and olives, blue water reflecting a bluer sky, and the lovely margin of the lake, where marble villas and white villages, each with its campanile, looked like giant swans peeping out of their verdant nests, combined to form a scene worthy of a poet's dream.

We stayed at Belaggio, which my kind companion thought the fairest spot in this land of beauty. The ripples of the lake broke absolutely against the walls of the Hotel Genazzini, and shoals of silver fishes darted about under the windows, waiting to be fed or caught. It was enough delight to sit upon the terrace and track the shadows flying across the water and up the chestnut slopes on the opposite shore, or, at eventide, to watch the red-orbed sun sink in golden glory behind the purpling hills above Menaggio. It was enough delight to follow the white-sailed boats reflected on the water, till boat and shadow looked like some great bird with outspread wings; to see the darkness stealing over land and lake, and the fire-flies light their tiny lamps amongst the oleander bushes, whilst the heavens became alive with blinking stars, and the moon rose behind the pine tops on the Ser-belloni Gardens, moon and stars to shine

again in the nether sky below the lake.
Whilst gazing on such changeful beauty,
I almost forgot this wicked world, and the
wicked man who had worked me so much
harm, and would try to work me more.

Hotel life was too public, and too expen-
sive now that my voice was no longer a
bank-note. We looked about for a quiet
villa, where I could forget and be forgotten.
The season was only commencing, and
there was a choice; but most of the houses
we visited were too large for our party,
and too costly for our purse. At last we
found one on the opposite shore more suited
to our modest wants. The villa was not
much more than a *châlet*, but it lay in an
enchanting spot. The garden, though not
large, was tumbled about in little hills and
dells; and a brook, falling in a murmuring
cascade over a rocky ledge behind the villa,
wandered through the camelias and oleanders till it passed into the lake under a
rustic bridge, which led to a boat-house

and a landing-place. On a slight eminence above stood a summer-house, in the form of a Greek temple, almost hidden in creeping roses, where I spent many delightful hours of idleness. The whole garden was a wilderness of flowers—camelias, magnolias, oleanders, cactuses, and aloes, growing in uncared-for luxuriance, and the ground under the trees was purple with wild cyclamen. If it had not been for the weeds, which almost choked the flowers, it might have been a scrap of Paradise. Our little domain was closed in on the western side by grand old chestnut trees and aromatic pines, amongst whose branches the lake-wind kept up a perpetual whisper, as soothing as the plash of the waterfall and the tinkle of the brook hurrying over painted pebbles to the lake between banks tremulous with fronds of maidenhair.

My mother and great-grandmother were charmed with our choice, and enjoyed the scenery as much as I did. The marchesa, who had been failing in strength for the last year, declared that the fresh air made her feel quite young. Alas! that it should only have been the flicker before the light went out!

It was impossible to persuade my mother that I was not seriously ill. She watched me with anxious eyes, and showed delighted surprise if I joined with animation in conversation or broke into a laugh. I took to my singing again with renewed energy, practising several hours daily. I began by making the temple by the lake-side my music-room but, finding that my songs attracted boaters to stop and listen, I retired to a cool marble seat near the waterfall, where my only audience were the green lizards, which peeped at me between the sprays of maidenhair. I was a happy child again, revelling in the beautiful nature round me, and finding it all the more beautiful from the contrast between the whispering trees and breezy hills and those of paint and canvas, amongst which

I had lived so much of late. I almost
thanked my pitiless lover for driving me
from the fictitious to the real.

Bertie was mad with indignation at the
treatment I had met with from the Duke of
Maladetta, and said that his hands itched
to give the dastardly Italian rascal a sound
thrashing. Much as I longed to see my
fiancé, I had peremptorily forbidden him to
come till I sent for him, as I did not wish
an encounter to take place between my two
lovers, thinking that English fists would
stand a poor chance against an Italian
stiletto..

Bertie Annesley, of course, kept up a
constant correspondence with me, from
which I learned that he had found all
that he hoped to find in the French
studio. He had learned to look at nature
through French glasses, and, in painting a
picture, to be a little reticent, and leave
something to the imagination; to use a
little mystery for medium, and poetry for

paint. He had studied to such good purpose that his picture not only was admitted
on its own merits into the Royal Academy,
but was sold on the opening day. The
critics nearly all noticed it as the work of
an artist unknown to fame, but one who
would not long remain so. They pronounced the landscape to be true to nature,
and yet full of suggestions, whilst the
figures were unconventional and poetical.
Bertie sent me cuttings from the various
papers, which praised his " Charcoal
Burners in the New Forest," and repeated
some of the pretty things said to him
by more than one Royal Academician. In
fact, his head was getting so turned that
the only way to set it straight was a
holiday. I was not for a moment to
imagine that he was going to take so long
a journey merely to see a little woman
with whom he had parted under the
beeches of the New Forest. Oh dear, no!
He had heard that Italy was the land for

an artist, full of warmth and colour ; that
the Italian lakes were made to be painted ;
that Como was the most beautiful of the
lakes ; that Cadenabbia was the sweetest
spot on Como ; and he believed there was
a villa, or a *châlet*, with the prettiest
garden on the lake, about a mile off, which
he was most anxious to see. He wanted
to paint a certain waterfall. He believed
there was a marble seat close by, and that
a nightingale sang there all the day long.

Such gaiety of heart was infectious. I
forgot that I had forbidden him to come to
me without an invitation. I ran into the
house, singing my merriest song, startling
the marchesa from her doze. She was
always dozing now. In my joy of heart to
think that I was so soon to see my own
true love, I kissed her fading cheek, and
arranged her pillow. She seemed pleased,
as well as surprised, at my attentions, and,
taking my hand in her own, begged me to
look after my mother when she was gone,

and never to allow her to return to the stage. I kissed her again, and promised to obey her wishes, saying at the same time that I hoped it would be long before I was called upon to act in her place.

"Not long, my child—not long," she said. "You are a good, dear girl. I can trust you to watch over your mother."

I thought the old lady was only feeling the first hot days, and told her that I was expecting a visitor, who would soon laugh her out of her low spirits. I went off to find my mother, and tell her my good news.

"He is coming here at once," I cried joyfully, "to Cadenabbia."

"Who?" she asked. "Not the duke, I see by your face."

"Bertie Annesley. He has sold his picture in the Academy, and is coming to see the Italian lakes."

"And some one who is living in a villa on the shore of one of them."

"Oh, mother! have you guessed my

secret?" I whispered, as I laid my head upon her shoulder to hide my blushes.

"I must have been very blind, my dear Nellie, if I had not discovered that you and Bertie Annesley were more than friends. I have often wondered why my child did not confide in her mother."

"I was afraid that you would object to my marrying a poor man. Now it is quite different. Bertie has sold his first picture, and will soon make a fortune."

"One swallow does not make a summer, Nellie. It is far more difficult to make money with the brush than you are perhaps aware of. Wealth only comes to great geniuses."

"Bertie is a great genius, mother."

"I hope he is. And so you are engaged to this paragon of painters?"

"Yes, mother, I am. I have loved Bertie for years."

"For years, Nellie! What an old woman you are—just one and twenty!"

"I have loved him ever since I saw him first, ten years ago, not exactly as I love him now, for then we were like brother and sister. You won't object to Bertie for a son-in-law, mother dear? I think you liked him when he came with us to Dover."

"I had not much opportunity of judging his character, but I thought him a most charming young man. If he is as good as he is handsome, you have an exceptional lover."

"He is indeed, mother—better than his looks—noble, generous, and, with all his strength, as tender as a child."

"I see you are very much in love, my Nellie; but you cannot live on love, though young things think they can. The Annesleys are very poor."

"Bertie will not be poor long, and I am making a good income by my singing."

"You *were*, dear child."

"Oh, don't remind me of that dreadful

man, just as I am thinking of one so different!"

"I hope we shall hear no more of the Duke of Maladetta, but I still cannot help feeling that you are unnecessarily frightened at the man. I could never see anything peculiar in his eyes, except their rather too open admiration for yourself."

"I cannot expect you or any one to understand their power over me. I believe that the duke could force me to do almost anything he willed, even to marry him, hating him as I do and loving another. Oh, mother, keep me out of his way! Save me from those dreadful eyes!" and I shuddered at the thought.

"You must fight against this nervous feeling. Be strong, and conquer it, dear child."

"I wish I could persuade you that this is not a case of nerves; I never was hysterical. If you won't believe me, Bertie will."

"Nerves or no nerves, I only want to see you well and happy, my child. We must wait for Dr. Annesley. I have much faith in his treatment. Write and tell him that he will be heartily welcomed by every one at the Villa Paulina, and not the least by Nellie's mother."

I was mute with happiness, and could only answer with a tender kiss.

I had not long to wait. A week later I was practising *roulades* and shakes, breaking now and then into some well-known aria, when I heard a step upon the gravel-path leading to the cascade. I should have known that step amongst a thousand. It was Bertie's firm but light footstep. I ran to meet him, and in a minute more was clasped to my darling's heart. How changed he was! He had grown big and broad, and wore a long silky beard. He looked like some grand Scandinavian god in the blonde beauty of his noble manhood. Whilst he was with me, I need have no fear of Italian dukes with magnetic eyes.

We sat together by the cool waterfall, and talked as lovers have talked, I suppose, ever since the days that Adam told his love to Eve in Eden. We talked of past days of happiness, and of still happier days to come, when we should meet to part no more. We talked of the progress we each had made in our respective professions. I told him of my many triumphs on the stage, whilst he was able to assure me that he would soon be able to offer me a home. He had more orders than he could get through for many months. I had never seen Bertie's eyes flash with rage till he made me tell him of the Duke of Maladetta's persecution and threat to ruin me, if I did not accept him for a husband; but we had so many pleasant things to discuss that we agreed to ignore the unpleasant ones.

I led Bertie, leaning on his arm, to the house, where my mother greeted him with

all the warmth I could have wished for.
The marchesa received him most graciously,
and asked, with a pleasant smile but feeble
voice, if this was the visitor who was to
restore her to health and spirits. She had
either heard my secret from my mother or
read it in my sparkling eyes, for she added
sotto voce that she was not surprised that,
with such a lover in England, I had not
looked with favour on the Duca di Maladetta's suit. For her part, she had a
preference for black hair and eyes ; but that
was a matter of taste. Bertie, who had
learnt Italian from his mother, knelt on
one knee by the invalid's sofa, and offered
to dye his hair any colour she fancied.
He did not see how he could change his
eyes from blue to black, unless she would
give him hers, which were the most beautiful he had ever seen. The marchesa tapped
his cheeks quite briskly with her fan, and
the two laughed and chatted together as
if they were old friends. In the evening

she told me that the arrival of my *inamo-rato*, who, for an Englishman, she thought nearly perfection, had done her more good than all the tonics she had been taking.

Tagliano also took an immediate liking to my *fiancé*; they seemed to understand each other at once, and to have very similar art theories. But, then, I had given Bertie several hints as to the peculiarities of the first violin.

Bertie at once dropped into our ways, liked our hours, our cooking—everything Italian. He spoke the language wonderfully well, considering how little he had studied it; and his mistakes made his conversation even more amusing than it would have been without them. He had the knack of creeping into every one's heart, and staying there. He seemed to carry sunshine with him, and to impart it to those around him.

The days passed rapidly in a delightful monotony of beauty and happiness. Bertie, who slept at the hotel at Cadenabbia, came in the cool of the morning to the villa, and joined in our *al fresco* breakfast. He and I spent the hot hours in my music-room, the little dell by the cascade. There I sang through my parts, except that of Margarita, which, for a time at all events, I had banished from my *repertoire*, as I could not hear the music without a shudder. Bertie brought his easel, and painted whilst I sang, making a lovely picture of the waterfall and the pool beneath. He placed me on a bank of maidenhair in the character of Ondine, with my feet dipping in the clear water.

In the evenings we were rowed upon the lake, peeping at all the beautiful gardens round the frequent villas, and finding new views of loveliness at every winding of the shore. It was the perfection of earthly enjoyment to glide over the sparkling ripples, the eyes satiated with the sight of nature in her sweetest garb and mood, the ears soothed with the

gurgling of the water beneath our boat and
the musical dip and drip of the oars, and
the heart filled with an absorbing love. We
were alone under the striped canopy, and
could talk without restraint, as the old
boatman did not know the language we
spoke. We talked of our love and the
home that we were soon to make in dear
old England ; we talked of the wealth that
was to pour from Bertie's brush, which I
wanted to increase by singing at Covent
Garden. But there Bertie was firm. I
was not to sing on any operatic stage when
he once called me wife. He knew that he
could make enough for both of us to live
on with comfort ; but, apart from that, his
uncle, to whom he had opened his heart, had
promised to allow him a settled income, so
that all he had to do on returning to England was to find a home and buy the ring.
He had told his mother, too, of our engagement, and had heard from her that our
marriage was the dearest wish of her heart.

For once, the course of true love seemed to be running with unproverbial smoothness. And when night dropped her spangled veil over the earth, and gave her time to sleep off the fever of the day, we, Bertie and I, sat together, hidden by the canopy from the oarsman's eye, and, hand in hand, my head upon his breast, dreamed in silence of our love—the happiest pair of lovers in creation.

It was a dream of bliss too sweet to last. Life cannot be all love-making, and Bertie felt that his holiday must soon be over. He must wake and work. I would not keep him in Capua. I would not if I could.

The day came for us to part, and in the little temple by the shore we took a tender farewell, whilst the boat waited at the marble steps below.

He left me in tears. Through the mist in my eyes I watched his receding boat. He sent me many kisses across the blue water, which I sent him back fourfold. At last he reached the steamer, which was to carry him to Colico. He waved his handkerchief from the deck. I watched the vessel growing smaller, till Bertie's signal became a white speck in the distance. A promontory hid both from my sight. There was nothing now to remind me of my loss but the wake left by the paddle of the steamer, and that soon died away.

Bertie was gone! How little did I think what troubles I should have to undergo before I saw his dear face again!

CHAPTER XIII.

AN ABDUCTION.

NOT caring to show my red eyes even to my mother, I sat down in my rose-bower, still watching the smoke of the steamer, which I could see floating in the air beyond the intervening tongue of land. I thought of the happy hours Bertie and I had been spending together on the shores and on the waters of beautiful Como, of the dear love he had given me, and of the sweet things he had whispered in my ear. And memory carried me back to the days when, boy and girl, we had wandered under the shade of the beeches and oaks in the New Forest, bird's nests and wild

flowers being the only treasures we looked
for. Now we were man and woman, both
eager for a prize in the world's race. Bertie
was well on the way to win one; I had
already won mine, but the prize had been
snatched from my grasp by a man with a
black heart. I was glad that he had not
come across Bertie's path, as there might
have been bloodshed. I shuddered when I
thought that it might have been Bertie's
blood that would have been spilt, and I
closed my eyes, as if to shut out so terrible
a sight. The burning eyes of my persecutor
seemed to flash on my darkened retinæ till
banished by those of my own true love—
blue as the heavens, and as pure. They
were as different as light from darkness, as
good from evil. And then I fell a-dreaming,
dreaming of the love that made me the
proudest woman in the universe, although
I was a nameless outcast from my father's
home.

The noise of heavy oars fell upon my ear,

but I did not lift my head to look at the
boat, which was passing so near my bower.
I did not remark that the oars were silent
till I heard stealthy footsteps on the path
leading from the landing-step to the temple,
where I was sitting in the shade of the
overhanging portico. I got up to see who
the intruders were, and in a moment was
seized by two men. One tied a silk handkerchief over my mouth to muffle my
screams, and the other threw a heavy cloak
round me. I was lifted off my feet and
carried rapidly down the slope to the lake
side. I was passed from their hands to
others, and laid on my back. I knew by
the gurgling sound of water at my ear
that I was in a boat. "Presto, presto!"
I heard some one shout; and by the rapid
plashing of the oars and the creaking of
the rowlocks I knew that we were flying
over the water as fast as strong arms could
pull us.

I made an attempt to rise, but was

pushed back. A man's voice warned me
not to move, as orders had been given to
throw me overboard if I made any disturb-
ance. I was foolish enough to be frightened
at the threat, and lay still. A cushion
was placed under my head, and I began to
feel that my body was being covered over
for purposes of concealment. From the
shape of the things piled over me, and the
pungent odour which penetrated the cloak
in which I was wrapt, I made up my mind
that they were melons, and that I was in
a market boat. I could not move hand
or foot from the superincumbent mass.
Though my head was outside the heap of
fruit, I could hardly breathe, and I implored
to be allowed some air. I promised to be
still and not speak if only the cloak might
be removed from my mouth. Some one
cut a hole in the cloth, and exposed my
mouth and nose; my eyes were still covered.

It seemed that we rowed on for hours.
Once my head was lifted and food, delicate

food, was placed in my mouth, and some
rare wine was held to my lips. The air
grew cooler and cooler, and at last it
became dark. Night had fallen on us, and
still on we rowed. Bertie had left me at
five o'clock. It would not be dark before
nine or ten. I calculated that we must
have been on the lake at least four hours—
it seemed more like twenty-four to me.

I began to feel the weight above me become lighter, and from the splashes in the
water I guessed that the melons were being
thrown into the lake. It was not a real
market-boat, or the fruit would not have
been wasted in this way. At last the oars
slackened, and the boat grounded on a
gravel shore. Almost as stiff as a corpse,
I was lifted out of the boat and placed in a
carriage. An arm was placed gently round
me. From the moment that I was carried
off, I was convinced that my abduction was
the work of the Duke of Maladetta. The
thought that I was in his power almost

drove me mad, but the bodily discomfort and absolute pain I was suffering in the boat kept me from realizing mentally the full danger of my position. I was persuaded now that it was the Duke's arms that supported me. He had not been in the boat, or I should have felt his presence, I think, though my eyes were covered.

I was now absolutely in his power. God only could save me from that devil in man's form. I cried to God aloud in my agony, as only those can cry who know that none can help them save He alone. A cruel laugh, the jeering laugh of Mephistopheles, rang in my ears. I was poor lost Margarita in the arms of a man-fiend.— Faust and his tempter combined. Worn out with fatigue, and in mental agony that no words of mine can describe, I swooned away.

I remembered nothing more till I came to myself in a splendid apartment. A dozen wax candles did little towards lighting it, on account of its size and height. I was lying in an antique bed of carved wood, richly gilded; the curtains were of blue silk, brocaded with wreaths of flowers in their natural colours. The walls were hung with the same silk. Mirrors, girandoles, and rare cabinets in the cinque-cento style, bespoke the fact that I was in a palace, evidently, I thought, one of the Maladetta palazzi. I looked about me at all the beautiful objects, and rubbed my eyes to see if I was not in a dream, and then all the horrors of my situation flashed across my brain. I wished, indeed, that I had been dreaming.

On a gilded chair by my bedside lay a rich dressing-gown; on the floor were a pair of slippers, velvet embroidered in seed pearls. Costly robes and the finest *lingerie* were scattered about in undesignedly artistic confusion. Nothing was wanting to satisfy the taste of the most exacting lady of fashion. I took this all in at a glance, and wished more than ever that it was a dream.

I was not alone. A woman was standing by the dressing-table. She was looking into a silver-mounted box. I could see the glitter of diamonds in her hands. She was evidently admiring the jewels in the casket. Were these the tempter's gems?

I could not shake off the idea that I was Margarita, but, with her example before me, I did not feel inclined to break into the Jewel Song.

I called to the woman, who started, and dropped what she held in her hand on the floor. It was a diamond *rivière*. It lay on the carpet like a fiery snake. She approached the bed. She was wonderfully handsome—a thorough Italian, with blue-black hair and dark lustrous eyes. They were bold, bad eyes, but very beautiful. She was dressed in a peasant's costume, but the materials were of the richest description. The pins in her hair were gold, and of rare workmanship. Was this woman to be my keeper? I should find no sympathy in her breast. I could see she was the wicked servant of a wicked master, and her duty was to aid in ruining me.

"Where am I?" I asked her.

"In a beautiful chamber in a beautiful house, signorina."

"Whose house?"

"In the house of a gentleman who is rich and noble, and handsome—-oh, so handsome! You are a lucky young lady."

"I am the most miserable girl in all the world! I have been carried off from my mother's house. She will die of grief when she finds me gone."

"Is she an Italian lady?"

"Yes; more Italian than anything else. She was born and bred in Italy."

"Then she will be proud to think that you have such a rich lover, signorina."

"Whoever your master is, he is base, miserably base, to persecute a poor girl who does not love him."

"I can't hear my dear master abused. He is a great nobleman. You will love him some day. Girls are silly things, and don't know their own minds."

"I know my mind well enough. I should despise and hate any man, if he were the King of Italy himself, who would stoop to carry off a girl against her will."

"You talk very finely, signorina; but you are not the first young lady who has talked so to me, and I have always found they cooed like turtle-doves after a time. My master has a wonderful talent for taming vixen."

"Your master will never tame me. He may imprison me, starve me, kill me, but tame me, never! He may break my heart, but not my will. I know who he is; he is the Duca di Maladetta. I believe he is the devil himself. No human being could be so vile, so mean, so——"

"Stop, signorina. I won't listen to such abuse of my kind lord."

" He may have been kind to you; he has been cruel, oh, so cruel to me ! " and I burst into tears.

I thought I heard the woman sigh. Could it be a sigh of sympathy ? I looked up, but the eyes were as cold as ever.

I rose from the bed and dropped into a luxurious chair. The woman pushed a table towards me laid for supper, and rang a bell. I was very hungry. A tray was brought to the door, the contents of which she placed before me. I wanted strength for the coming struggle, and did not refuse to partake of the rich fare provided. I was rather afraid that the wine might be drugged, and asked the woman to drink some. She smiled, and tossed off a full glass.

Hunger satisfied and thirst quenched, I said that I would retire for the night. The woman offered to brush my hair. I was to understand that she was my waiting-maid.

" And my warder," I added.

She insisted on seeing me to bed. I let her have her way. Before she left me, she showed me the bell, and explained the door-bolt. She bade me a civil good night. I was alone—alone with my sorrow and my fears.

CHAPTER XIV.

A LUXURIOUS PRISON.

I BOLTED the door, and went to the window. I looked out into the night. The moon was large and lustrous. Beneath me I could hear the rustle of the night wind in the trees. They were pines, and evidently grew on the steep side of a hill. The house was very large. I could see an expanse of white walls and many windows with shutters. There was a story between me and the deep overhanging eaves. The tops of the umbrella pines almost came up to my window. There must have been one if not two floors below me. I was a captive without a hope of escape—from my window, at least. In the distance I saw a silver streak; it was water, probably the lake of Como.

I shut the window and went round the room, tapping the walls to see that there were no secret doors, no sliding panels. I could find no indication of any. My limbs were bruised and aching. My mind was as weary as my body. Sleep I must, and after a fervent prayer for help and protection for myself, and for a blessing on those I loved, some of whom must be in terrible anxiety on my behalf, I slept the sleep of worn-out nature.

The sun was shining into my room when I woke from my long and unbroken slumber. I could now see the vastness of the chamber and the beauty of the rococo furniture and fittings. I was wide awake and rested. All the circumstances of my abduction came vividly into my mind, and I pictured to myself the commotion and distress at home, when they found I was absent from the evening meal.

A knock at the door interrupted my sad reverie. I asked who was there. "Mariuccia, your waiting-maid," was the answer. I opened the door and let her in. By daylight she did not look so bold. Her eyes did not flash so brightly; her dress was less rich in texture, and she looked more like a peasant. She insisted on helping me to dress, and wanted me to wear one of the many beautiful costumes lying about. I spurned them from me, and refused to put on anything but my own tumbled frock. When my toilette was completed, she told me that breakfast was waiting for me in my boudoir next door.

I could not help admiring the beautiful little room. The walls were white and gold, the panels being filled with mirrors, on which were painted, behind the glass, festoons of flowers carried by flying cupids. The ceiling was alive with hovering Loves, the work of some masterhand. The furniture was after the taste of the Louis XIV.

period, the chairs and fauteuils being covered with tapestry. The fresh bright hill air came in through the open window. I looked out at the glorious landscape. I pointed to a distant town at the head of the lake, and asked if it was Colico.

" No, signorina, Lecco," Mariuccia answered ; and then, seeming to regret what she had said, added, " at least, I think so."

" And that town on a hill in the far distance ? "

She shook her head, and would not reply.

" You have been told not to gratify my curiosity. Never mind. As that is Lecco, and we are looking south, I can name the place without your help. It is Bergamo. I was singing there last year."

" You are an opera-singer ? "

" Yes. That is how I met the Duca di Maladetta."

" I thought you were a lady."

" So I am."

"I mean a great lady. You look like one."

"My great-grandmother is the Marchesa Castracane, and my father is an English baronet."

"Then you are half English. I thought you were not much of an Italian. English ladies are very prudish, are not they, signorina?"

"They are good, honest women. The men, too, are honourable; and such a thing as abduction is unknown. A man like your duke would be hooted out of the country."

"You can tell him so, if you like; but I will not listen to anything against him. He is my master, and I——" She stopped dead short.

Now that I knew the town by the lake was Lecco, and not Colico, as I thought, I saw that I had been rowed across the lake, and down the branch of the Lago di Como called the Lago di Lecco. I had

seen it from the Serbelloni Gardens, blue
peeps through the pines and cypresses, but
had never sailed on it   I had some idea
of the situation of my luxurious prison.   I
could turn my eyes in the direction of
Cadenabbia, and fly in fancy over the steep
promontory of Belaggio to our villa on the
opposite shore.   A picture came before me
again of the trouble caused by my mysterious disappearance—my mother looking
distractedly for traces of her lost daughter,
Tagliano going for the police, the boatmen
perhaps dragging the lake for my body, all
in sorrow, anxiety, dismay.   They would
not find any footsteps on the gravel-path.
There had been no struggle near the
temple, and water keeps no traces.

My great hope was that they would
telegraph at once for Bertie.   He could
not have gone far on his homeward journey.
A telegram would catch him at Chiavenna,
or somewhere on the Splugen Pass.   Surely
their suspicions would fall on the Duke of

Maladetta. The police would suggest an abduction, and search all his palaces; this one first, as it was the nearest. This thought gave me a little hope, and I rose from breakfast somewhat comforted. I went back to the window, and gazed on the smiling landscape—on one side, a rolling sea of hills and mountains, purpling in the distance; on the other, a rich champaign dotted with blue lakes, with here and there a white village peeping out of the vines and olives.

As I sat and gazed, a sudden thrill ran through me, like the shock of an electric battery. Involuntarily I turned round. The Duke of Maladetta was standing at the half-opened door.

"May I have permission to pay my respects to my fair guest?" he asked, in a voice half deference, half victory.

"A gaoler may visit his prisoner without asking leave," I answered; "but even a gaoler would knock at the door of a cell tenanted by a woman."

" The door was ajar, and I thought you had left the room. But when I saw your beautiful pose, my artistic eyes could not help admiring the graceful outlines against the light. I stood for a minute in silence. Forgive the intrusion. May I come in ? I have much for which to crave forgiveness."

" You have, indeed ! You have treated me as woman was never treated, except by a brigand."

" I cannot deny it. But life was too short and love too strong to suffer me to live and love you at a distance. I was cruel to be kind."

" Cruel to me, kind to yourself."

" I want to be kind to you, if you will let me. I love you as woman was never loved before."

" By you ! " I added, with a look of contempt.

" Sarcasm does not sit well on those sweet lips, Nella mia."

" I am not your Nella ; I am only your prisoner."

" Fair prisoner, then, if you will have it so, I love you to distraction. I offer you again my rank, my wealth, my love. I am ready to present you to the world as my duchess. Can I pay you a greater compliment ? "

" I do not deny the compliment. I do not say that the offer is not honourable, the position offered not high, the fortune not colossal ; but there is one objection which ought to satisfy a gentleman, a nobleman—I do not love you."

" I would make you love me, Nella. I have the happy faculty of inspiring love."

" Not the love I value. You could never make me love you—never ! "

" Only let me try. I have brought you here to make you love me. I have never failed before. You will learn to love me, if you will only give your heart fair play ;

if you will let it meet my heart unpre-
judiced."

" You forget that my heart is not mine.
It belongs to another."

" Curse the man that has come between
us."

" He did not come between you and me ;
he was there before I ever saw your face."

" I will teach you to forget him."

"Never ! You can kill my body, but
you cannot kill my love."

" We shall see. At all events, possession is nine points of the law, and I have
you safe in my keeping. No one, not
even this fine English lover of yours, can
snatch you away from me now."

" Do not be so sure of that. My mother's
suspicions will naturally fall on you, and
the police are probably now on my track."

" The signora may have her suspicions,
but they will not help her."

" Your palaces are well known. They
will search them one after the other. This

is the nearest. They will come here first."

"They will never look for you here. You must think very poorly of my abilities, if you imagine that I should have been fool enough to bring you to a house belonging to myself."

"This is not one of your villas?"

"Of course not! I have hired it expressly for you. It was taken in another man's name. No one has any idea that the Duke of Maladetta has anything to say in the transaction. I came here in disguise, and the servants I have with me are mine, body and soul."

My last hope was gone. I turned deadly sick with despair and terror. Those cruel eyes were upon me, and I quailed before them.

"Why are you frightened at me, Nella?" he went on, in the sweet singing voice that he could assume at times. "I only wish you well. I love you, mio dolce amor; why should I want to harm you? I spoke to you like a madman at Florence. I behaved like a brute to you at Naples. I do not deserve that my love should be returned. Let me try and make amends for the past. I humbly ask your pardon, and promise never to offend again."

"The only amends you can make is to let me go home at once," I sobbed.

"The fowler does not liberate the bird the moment he has caught it. No, signorina; you are safe in the net, and here you will stay—till you love me."

"That will be till my death."

"Well, till you marry me, I will say."

"I will never marry where I do not love."

"Then you had better make haste to love me, as you will be my wife before long. In the mean time, remember, everything here is at your disposal. Think of me only as your slave—the slave of a very cruel queen."

" Queen of a prison, where the queen is a captive and the slave the gaoler."

" Still sarcastic, bella donna. I see you are tired. I only regret that I am the cause of your fatigue. I will relieve you of my company, and wish you a pleasant rest."

" I am not in the least tired, thank you."

" Then you wish me to stay and amuse you."

" Certainly not. I shall be in suffering as long as your eyes are upon me."

" Then I will make my bow, signorina ; but before I go, let me set your mind at rest on one point. You are as safe here as in your mother's house. No one shall annoy you, least of all the host, who adores you. He hopes to be allowed the privilege of visiting you now and then, when you are weary of solitary confinement. It is needless to repeat that my intentions are strictly honourable. I mean you to become my wife voluntarily. We shall be married before a priest in a chapel with legal witnesses. There shall be no possibility of a doubt that you are my duchess. I give you ten days to make up your mind to take me quietly for your husband. If you are still obstinate, I shall use my influence to lead you to the altar, and exact an unwilling 'Yes' when the priest asks if you will take me as your husband. Remember Naples and the San Carlo. If I can make you silent, I can also make you speak. A rivederli, signorina."

I felt the duke had not exaggerated his power. He could force me to take the marriage vow against my will, and he would force me. My only hope was in escape or rescue. One seemed as unlikely as the other.

Poor me! Poor Bertie!

CHAPTER XV.

MISTRESS AND MAID.

THE days dragged on, but I did not blame them for their slowness. I wished that those ten days might have stretched into ten years. The duke visited me daily, alternately imploring me to love him and threatening compulsion if I refused—now kind, now brutal. He was never two minutes together in the same mood, and would jump from one extreme to the other and back again a dozen times in the same visit. There was a versatility in his mental organization which astonished me.

He evidently was persuaded that he was treating me with exceptional kindness and condescension in offering me marriage. He assured me it was the first time that he had ever dreamt of treating a woman with such deference. He said that I was not like the rest of my sex, and that there was a moral halo about me that lifted me above all other women, and rendered it impossible for him to treat me as he had treated scores of others. If he was treating me with unwonted respect, God help his other victims!

A week passed, seven days out of the ten of comparative freedom. No change came over my feelings towards my host, except that I loathed and feared him more as I felt his influence gaining ground. I was like the poor animal fascinated by the boa constrictor. I could not move away from the serpent's cruel eyes, or help watching the writhings of the slimy coils that were soon to encircle me and crush my life out.

In three days I was to be married in the chapel of the villa. The priest was in the house, the duke told me; the lawyer would arrive early on our wedding-day with the settlements and witnesses. I should then become his own dear wife, the wife who was to make him good and happy. I was an angel, he repeated, sent to turn him to better things, and his marriage with me would open the gate of heaven, which he had thought to be closed against him for ever. On this occasion he spoke with tears in his eyes, and I felt that his love must be genuine. If it had not been that I had given my heart so entirely to another, the idea of saving the duke's soul might have had some extenuating influence over my repugnance for the man. A little pity began to mingle with my disgust and dread. Was this a part of the magnetism at work on me? I asked myself. Only three days more, and Bertie and I would be separated for ever in this world. My heart was breaking; but I saw no escape from the inevitable.

On entering my bedroom that night, I
found a large packing-case on the floor.
It was addressed to me. I supposed it to
be a present from my ducal lover. I had
had enough of his presents, and too much
of his admiration. I did not think of
opening the case; whatever it contained,
it could have no interest for me. Mariuccia's
curiosity, however, was so great that she
begged to be allowed to open it. I told
her she might do what she liked, and keep
the contents of the box, so far as I was
concerned. I turned away, and was letting
my hair down at the dressing-table. Suddenly a cry rang through the room. I
looked round. Mariuccia was on her knees
before the open case. Her hands were
clenched in an agony of rage and grief,
her face was distorted, her great black
pupils dilated and flashed with fire. She
rose to her full height, and looked at me
with a devil in her eyes.

"It is a wedding-dress," she hissed, "a

bridal wreath and veil! Are you going to marry the duke in earnest?"

"He says so; and, if he says so, you know he will make me."

"Do you love him, signorina?"

"I hate him."

"Then, you do not wish to be his wife?" she asked, the anger disappearing from her face.

"The very idea is killing me; but there is no escape. The priest is in the house, and I am to be dragged to the altar the day after to-morrow."

"You are not deceiving me? You do not wish to become his duchess?"

"I have refused him over and over again—first at Florence, and every day since I was brought to this prison house. He has given me ten days to see if I will alter my mind, and marry him voluntarily. If I refuse, he says that he will force me, by some secret power he possesses, to become his wife."

"You are an Englishwoman, and the English always speak the truth. If an Italian had told me that she refused to marry the Duke of Maladetta, I should have said she lied. The duke has offered to marry you? He loves you?"

"He says he does, and I almost believe him."

"He loves such a pale-faced thing as you!" cried my waiting-maid, with more sincerity than politeness. "He loves you with an honest love!"

"He tells me that I am the first woman who has inspired him with a genuine love."

"He told you that! the liar, the fiend!" and her eyes flashed again with fury. "He used to love me once. He drew me from a happy home with his fine promises. Ah! he really loved me then. If I had only been a lady, and not a poor peasant girl, I might have kept his love. I gave him all my love. I love him still. He has made me what you see I am, the slave of his iniquities. But I cannot tear myself away, because I love him with such a love that heaven would be hell without it, and hell would be heaven to me if he only loved me."

"Poor Mariuccia! He loved you once! How long has he ceased to love you?"

"He loved me longer than he ever loved any other woman," she answered proudly. "He loves me enough now to keep me always near him."

"You do not wish me to be his wife, Mariuccia?"

"If he marries you, I will either kill myself or you."

"Then, why not help me to escape? For God's sake, help me! If you do not, he will force me to marry him. Save me, Mariuccia!" and I threw my arms round her neck.

"It is impossible, signorina. There is only one way out of the castle, and that is watched."

" Could you post a letter for me to bring my friends to my rescue ? "

" I could try," she answered hesitatingly.

" It must be posted before the morning ; we have only one free day."

" I think it might be done. My room is near the ground under the pines. One of the *gardes champêtres* often comes to my window for a chat. He is coming to-night. He wants to court me. I let him come, for he brings me news of the outer world. It is well to have a friend to fetch and carry."

" Could he not help me to escape by your window ? "

" The window is heavily barred."

" The bars might be cut, Mariuccia."

" Your escape would be traced to me, and I should have to pay the penalty with my life. No, no! write your letter at once, and it shall be posted before midnight. It is only ten o'clock now."

" What is the name of this house ? "

" The Villa Altamonte. It belongs to
the young Duco d'Altamonte. Everybody
knows the house ; it is the largest in these
parts. It is six miles from Lecco, and
twelve from Bergamo."

Oh, the joy of returning hope, hope
abandoned! My heart beat so fast that I
could hardly breathe. There was no paper
or ink in the room. Mariuccia left me to
fetch some from her own room. How slow
she was! It seemed as if she would never
bring the writing materials. There was
not a moment to be lost. I almost feared
that it was already too late to hope that a
letter would reach my mother in time.
Perhaps she had returned to Florence to
look for me there. I must write to the
villa in Como and to the Palazzo Castracane. It was only my impatience that
magnified Mariuccia's delay. She was
back again before five minutes had expired.
She was able to tell me that her friend was
under her window, and had promised to

run the whole distance to Lecco, and put the letters in the box before the midnight post went out.

I wrote the letters as fast as my trembling hand would let me. I told my mother that I had been abducted by the Duke of Maladetta, and was his prisoner in the Villa Altamonte, which he had hired in a false name. I described the appearance and position of the house, high on the hillside. above the pine woods. I went on to say that my marriage was fixed for the following Wednesday, this being Monday night, and that my rescuers must be in time to prevent my going to the altar at noon on that day, as I felt that the duke's magnetic power would force me to take the marriage vows against my will. At Mariuccia's suggestion, I added that a *garde champêtre*, with an eagle's feather in his cap, would be on the landing-stage at Lecco from five o'clock on the following afternoon; that he would be in my confidence, and would

communicate the plans settled on for my
rescue. I said, further, that the rescuing
party must not be less than twenty in
number, as there were several men in the
house, who would obey the duke's orders
to the death. Mariuccia took my letters to
her faithful admirer, who promised to return in the morning for her final directions.

She and I sat up and talked far into the
night. Indeed, the eastern sky was rosy
when we said "Buona notte." Our plans
were settled, not exactly to my satisfaction,
but to hers. I had tried to persuade her
to fly with me. I offered her a home, and
painted as brightly as I could the happiness
of a better life away from the thraldom of
her wicked master. But she still loved
the man who had ruined her and made her
his slave, and would rather be his *âme
damnée* than find salvation away from his
presence. When I found that she would
not accept my proposal, I suggested that
the window bars should be cut soon after

dark on Tuesday night, and that I should escape by myself in time to allow them to be refixed before daylight. This seemed the easiest and safest plan of escape. But she would not hear of it. She gave no reasons against it, but simply negatived the suggestion.

Mariuccia wished that my rescuers should be admitted into the house through her window, and that the bars should be replaced as soon as they were inside. She would lead them to the chapel, and conceal them behind the old tombs of the Altamontes. I did not like the idea. I did not wish the chapel to be desecrated by a conflict—a conflict which might possibly result in the defeat of my rescuers—who knows, in the death of some of them, and Bertie might be amongst the number. But I saw that my only chance of escape was to trust entirely to her, and thwart her in nothing. I ceased at once to argue the question, and accepted her proposals.

I think she wished to be convinced of the duke's real intention to make me his wife, and, when convinced, that her vengeance should overtake him at the steps of the altar, where he was about to seal his love to another which had been plighted to her. In her desire for revenge, she forgot that the separation between her and her false lover would be as great as if she had fled with me; that is, if the part she had taken in my rescue were discovered —a contingency which, I suppose, did not occur to her. There is a great deal of the theatrical in the Italian character, and Mariuccia forgot everything but the *coup de théâtre* she was arranging.

We were just about to part when a sudden idea flashed across my brain. I jumped up from my chair, and, standing by the side of Mariuccia, looked into a mirror. She seemed strangely puzzled at this eccentric performance.

" We are exactly the same height!" I cried excitedly.

"What has that to say to the matter?"

"You could wear my wedding-dress, and be married in my place."

The suggestion seemed to take away Mariuccia's breath. Her eyes flashed for a moment with a look of triumph, and then fell.

"No, no! that would never succeed. I am dark as night, and you are as fair as a lily."

"The veil is thick;" and I ran to fetch it.

It was a priceless veil of rare old Pointe de Venise; evidently a family relic— probably the bridal veil of generations of Maladettas. It was so covered with floral designs that the face could hardly be seen through it. I threw it over my head and looked in the mirror.

"I should not know myself," I cried.

"I can see your hair; it shines through the lace like gold. No, it would never do!"

"Nonsense, Mariuccia! I did not think

you would be so easily frightened. Tell me one thing. Would you like to take my place, and become the wife of the Duke of Maladetta ? "

" It would be the grandest revenge that woman ever worked. He might kill me, but I should die an honest woman—his wife, the Duchess of Maladetta." And then her voice changed from the harsh tones of gratified revenge and ambition to a soft, sweet murmur. " Perhaps his love might come back when he found that he was bound to me—that I was his wife. He loved me once, signorina. Yes; he loved me dearly once."

" Perhaps it might," I answered. " Indeed, I wish it might, as you love him so. Will you make the venture ? Remember, ' Nothing venture, nothing gain.' "

" I think I will," she answered hesitatingly; and, after a pause, continued with a firm voice, " Yes, I will."

" Then let us put our heads together, and

see if two women cannot outwit one man, though that man is the Duke of Maladetta."

" You cannot change the colour of my hair."

" If there were time, it would be easy. There are washes which turn the darkest hair light as mine ; but we have no time to send to Milan for a bottle."

" If we could get the wash, it would not do to dye my hair. If I was to be absent when the lawyer sends for you, the duke might ask why you came without me."

" Well, then, I will cut off my back hair, and make you a front."

" If the lawyer is to be here at ten o'clock, and the wedding is fixed for mid-day, as you say, there will be no time for cutting off your hair and making it up for me. No, it cannot be ; " and she sighed pitifully.

Suddenly my eyes fell upon a robe of golden satin lying on a chair. I fetched it, and matched it against my hair. It was

all but the same shade. I saw Mariuccia's
eyes beam with intelligence and satisfaction. I put the veil over the satin. The
effect was perfect.

" There is plenty of golden hair for you,
Mariuccia ! "

" That is more like it. But my skin is
so dark."

" There are cosmetics on the dressing-
table enough for a harem. *Poudre de riz*
will turn you into a lily, as you call me.
Will you make the attempt ? "

" I will. I can but fail, and he can only ·
kill me once."

" You will not fail. To-morrow I will
make you a satin wig. I will copy all my
plaits, and fasten some real curls on the
brow. Cheer up, Mariuccia; you shall be
Duchess of Maladetta. When you are, you
will be such a grand lady that you will
have nothing more to say to poor Nella
Bardi, the opera-singer."

" I shall kneel at her feet and beg for a

little of her love, as I kneel and beg for it now ; " and Mariuccia fell on her knees, reminding me of a picture of a beautiful magdalen by Guido, in the Pitti Palace.

"You are saving me from worse than death," I answered, raising her from the ground. "You have already earned my gratitude and love."

CHAPTER XVI.

IN THE CHAPEL OF THE ALTAMONTE VILLA.

ALL had been arranged with Carlo, the *garde champêtre*, who little thought that he was working for love of one who would never return his love, that he was working, indeed, to marry her to another. We must hope that his heart was not very deeply engaged, and that the reward for my rescue would make up to him in some measure for his disappointment.

He was to meet my rescuers, whoever they might be, on Tuesday evening, on the steamboat pier at Lecco, and to bring them to Mariuccia's window before daylight. There would be a three-quarter moon after midnight, but there was no fear of the party being seen from the villa, as they would ascend the hill under cover of the pines, which grew right up the steep, almost precipitous, incline on which the villa stood, and swept the walls with their branches. A blacksmith, well paid for secrecy, was to remove the bars during the night, and replace them as soon as the party were inside the window. A stout ladder was in readiness to help them to enter without noise or difficulty, though the window was not more than six feet from the ground.

Tuesday was to me a day of deep anxiety and suspense. Would my letter reach my mother by the early post? Would there be time to get together twenty men to form the rescuing party? Would Bertie be amongst the number? Whilst my thoughts were alternating between hope and fear, I occupied my fingers in making the covering for Mariuccia's black hair. I cut a piece out of the skirt of the golden satin robe, and fitted a skull cap over her hair, and rolled round it plaits of satin, in imitation of my own. Under the veil the illusion was perfect. Mariuccia was even in greater excitement than I was. She was constantly trying on her satin wig, and complaining that it made her skin look so dark. To set her mind at rest, I powdered and rouged her till she became a blonde. My theatrical experience naturally aided me much to secure a complete make-up.

The duke paid me his usual morning visit in my boudoir, and stayed longer than usual. That was my fault, as I received him more kindly, and let him think that my aversion was passing away. He seemed really rejoiced at the sudden change, and assured me that he would only live to make me a happy wife. He promised me everything that riches could give—jewels, fine dresses, equipages, an honoured place amongst the highest nobility in Italy, and a cordial reception at Court. I smiled to myself as I thought how little I cared for the attractions he dangled before me in comparison with Bertie's love, and how the biter would be bit when he found that I had escaped the snare and left another bird in my place.

The duke naturally misinterpreted my smile, and was encouraged to take my hand, which I hypocritically allowed to remain a short time in his, hoping to lure him into a fool's paradise, and to lull any suspicions that I was not prepared to take my place by his side at the altar on the following day. I felt I was acting almost wickedly in deceiving a man who, I believed, really loved me in his own selfish way; but at the same time it was a glorious thing that Margarita should cozen Mephistopheles. If I succeeded, the tables would indeed be turned. I was playing a dangerous game, and that made it all the more fascinating to play.

The duke left me, mightily pleased with himself and with me. He kissed my hand gallantly, and whispered in his sweetest voice, " À demain." I could not help laughing outright, when the door was closed and he was gone, at the thought of what a very unpleasant "à demain" it would be for him. To-morrow I should be free, and he bound. " À demain, Monsieur le Duc; à demain ! "

I hardly closed my eyes all night. I was constantly getting up and opening the window to listen for footsteps in the pine grove. There was not a sound but the nightingales in a copse to the left. I fancied I saw a light through the needles of the pines, and was sure it was the beacon lamp in Mariuccia's window. Now and again I heard a slight rasping noise, which I thought must be the black-smith's file at work on the iron bars. Tired with waking and watching, my head dropped on the cushioned window-sill, and

I fell into a sound sleep, from which I did not wake till Mariuccia knocked at my door. The moment I saw her smiling face, I knew that all was right. She told me that a party of twenty men were already hidden in the chapel, and that amongst them were two Englishmen—one, beautiful as the morning, with bright blue eyes and yellow hair ; the other, older, but a fine-looking gentleman. I recognized the portrait of my *fiancé*, and was happy. I wondered who his English companion could be.

I rose in wild spirits to think that my true love and I were under the same roof, and that before long I should be in his arms again. I was too elated to remember that there was much to be gone through before that happy moment. The wedding-dress was to be put on. It was wonderful how well it fitted, considering that the duke had nothing to guide him in giving the order except his eyes, unless he had

bribed my Florence dressmaker to give
him a pattern. The case had come from
Paris, from a *couturière* of celebrity. I
smiled at myself in the mirror. The
white dress suited me, and my heart
danced as I thought that before long I
should wear such a costume, though not so
costly a one, as Bertie's bride. Mariuccia
brought my breakfast into my bedroom ;
and before the hour fixed for the signing
of the settlements, I was sitting in my
boudoir, with my bridal wreath and veil
on, and a magnificent bouquet of white
orchids in my hand, which the duke had
sent me with his love.

The duke came punctually to seek me,
and led me on his arm down the grand
staircase. It was the first time that I had
seen any other portion of the villa than my
own apartments. It was hard to take in
the details through my thick veil, but I
made out that the hall was of magnificent
proportions. The walls were of coloured

marbles, and huge marble columns supported a gallery and the roof. I walked
lightly down the white marble stairs, for
my heart was no longer heavy. Mariuccia
followed, holding up my train. Who
would hold up her train when she took
my place? This thought suddenly flashed
through my mind, and made me feel that
all was not such plain sailing as I could
have wished. Turning round, I asked
Mariuccia to place my train over my arm,
and to fetch a handkerchief which I had
left in my room. She looked puzzled, but
obeyed. I wanted to manage my own
train, that she might do the same later,
without calling attention to the absence of
a maid.

On entering a magnificent saloon leading
out of the hall, I let my train down rather
ostentatiously, and shook it out to its full
length, and crossed the polished granite
floor, which was covered with arabesque
designs in brilliant colours, powdered lapis

lazuli and coral being used largely in the composition. The walls were painted in fresco with scenes from Homer; at least, I imagined so from one where, men in armour were climbing out of a great wooden horse surrounded by battlements, which I took to be those of Troy. I had time to observe all this, whilst the lawyer was reading out the deed of settlement.

The duke and I were seated, like a king and queen, on two gilded chairs or thrones. I could not help smiling to myself, as I thought it only wanted a ballet to make the scene really operatic. The duke was the tenor, I the soprano, and I wondered why the notary did not sing his part as bass. I listened with only half an ear, as the settlements did not affect me; but I heard enough to understand that the duke had settled on me a princely fortune, a palace at Naples, another at Genoa, and a villa on the Lago Maggiore. The duke asked if I was satisfied. I muttered my

thanks, and said that I was not worthy of
such munificence. He kissed my hand
gallantly, and assured me that if he was
King of Italy he would have laid his
kingdom at my feet. We signed the
document before the notary and witnesses.
The duke then led me back to my room,
where I begged that he would not return
to fetch me for the marriage service, but
meet me on the altar steps. It was ac-
cordingly settled that the notary should
attend me from my room to the chapel—
an arrangement which was thoroughly
satisfactory to me.

Once in my room, I threw off veil and
wreath, took off my bridal dress, and was
soon waiting on my waiting - maid.
Mariuccia and her mistress had changed
places. The dress fitted her fairly well.
The veil hid all defects, as it fell almost
to the feet. The get-up was complete.
It would have deceived the most astute.
The golden wig was perfect, softened over

the forehead by some curls which I had cut from my own head. The complexion matched the hair, and there was nothing to hint that it was not myself, except the black eyes, and these I instructed Mariuccia to keep modestly on the ground.

Being desirous of assisting at the ceremony, I had been shown by Mariuccia a door, which opened into a private gallery, or pew, looking down upon the chapel, where the family were accustomed to attend mass, without descending to the lower floor. There I should be able to see without being seen, and be safe if a struggle took place, in the event of my rescuers being discovered by the duke's menials. Mariuccia was very silent as to the course she intended to pursue when the marriage knot was tied. She seemed to be intentionally concealing her plans from me, but anxious that I should be present at the service, if quite out of the way of danger. I was prepared for a

scene of some sort, and looked forward
with a feeling of frightened pleasure to
being witness of the duke's discomfiture
and Mariuccia's triumph.

The clock struck twelve. My heart beat
louder at every stroke. Mariuccia was
perfectly self-possessed. She fell on her
knees and kissed my hands. I kissed her
on her forehead, and thanked her again
and again for saving me from a lifelong
misery. She left me, and went into the
adjacent boudoir. I heard the notary
come for her, and the rustle of her silks
as he led her from the room. I peeped
out, and saw her following her companion,
the train over her arm, as I had instructed
her how to place it.

As she descended the marble stairs, I
crept on tiptoe to the family pew. Hiding
myself behind some velvet hangings, I
looked down into the chapel. The sun
came in through the rich painted windows,
casting rainbow shadows on the chequered.

floor and marble monuments. The altar
was blazing with wax candles, and the air
was heavy with the scent of incense and
of orange blossoms, with which the floor
was thickly strewn. As much preparation
had been made for the ceremony as if
royalty had been expected to be present.
I appreciated the compliment, and gave
one thought of pity to the man who said
he loved me—but only one. He was
standing on the altar steps, waiting for
the bride.

A flush of pride and pleasure passed
over his handsome face as the bride appeared. She had dropped her train at the
chapel door, and walked up the aisle with
steady step and downcast eyes. What an
actress she would have made! She had
copied my gait to the life. I could hardly
believe that I was not looking at my own
double. I had studied walking and carriage professionally, and here was an un-
taught peasant who had picked up the

deportment that I had been at so much pains to acquire simply from watching me. She was as self-possessed as if she were going to meet a willing bridegroom. She had a good excuse for keeping her eyes out of sight in the bouquet, of which she was inhaling the perfume.

As she approached the altar, the duke advanced a few steps, and led her to the cushion on which she was to kneel, and took another by her side. The priest was standing before them in gorgeous robes, and acolytes in crimson cassocks swung silver censers round the kneeling pair. The service commenced, and choristers chanted a sweet Gregorian. It must have been the first time for many a day that the Duke of Maladetta went through the form of prayer. "The devil in the house of God," I said to myself, with a shudder, as I thanked the Almighty that I was not kneeling by his side.

I looked round the chapel whilst the

service proceeded, and thought I could see
the heads of my rescuers, who were crouch-
ing behind the tombs where the Altamontes
lay in marble sleep under Gothic canopies
of open fret-work; but the light was not
strong enough in the remote corners where
the tombs were erected to enable me to
discover Bertie's curly locks.

The service was over. The duke and
Mariuccia were man and wife, never again
to be divided, except by the hand of death.
The duke offered his arm to lead away his
bride. She hesitated to take it. What
was Mariuccia's purpose? Why had she
hidden my friends in the chapel? When
was I to be rescued? not till she had
declared herself? I had not long to wait
for an answer to my interrogative thoughts.
She stepped back a couple of steps, and
lifted her veil. Throwing off the wreath
and satin cap to which it was attached, she
stood in her own black hair. Her eyes
flashed triumphantly, looking all the larger

and darker from the white powder round them. The duke stood for a moment as one struck by a cruel blow. I almost pitied him ; for it must have been a bitter disappointment to find that it was Leah, not Rachel, that he had wedded. He stared as if he was stricken dumb, and then gave a cry of rage that I shall never forget to my dying day. The bride stood calmly triumphant, and smiled at her lord and master.

"Mariuccia!" at length he shrieked, whilst the white foam came to his lips, "Mariuccia, you have played me a scurvy trick. You think you have outwitted me, do you, daughter of Satan? Ha, ha! The Dukes of Maladetta do not mate with earth's vermin, such as you. I deny the marriage."

"It is too late for that, signor duca," she exclaimed calmly. "You have taken me to wife in the sight of God and before witnesses. You took every care that your marriage should be legal, and nothing now can break the knot the priest and the Church have tied."

"Fool! idiot! What do I care for God or Church! These men, priest, and notary, and witnesses, are all my creatures. They will do my bidding, and they will deny the marriage. What will your word be worth? Who will believe what you say, vile woman? Even if you could find a character, a low-born peasant such as you are would not have much chance of being listened to when the Duke of Maladetta calls you liar. I will accuse you of perjury, and see you lodged in a convict's cell! A fine bride, indeed! You did not marry this woman to me, did you, reverend father?"

"Not if you wish to deny the marriage," answered the priest. "I am here only to obey your orders."

"There, my fine duchess! And now I will ask the notary and his men whether

they know anything of a legal union between me and this masquerading Jezebel?"

"We know of no such union. There
are no legal proofs of any marriage that
we are aware of," answered the notary for
himself and his clerks.

"Ha, ha! my beautiful bride, my proud
duchess! what do you say now? Where
is your marriage certificate? Where are
your witnesses?"

"Here!" cried twenty voices, as Bertie
Annesley and his rescuing party rose up
on all sides from behind tombs and out of
corners hidden by marble columns. "We
are witnesses to the marriage of the Duke
of Maladetta to that lady standing there."

The men were all armed I knew, by the
ring of their guns upon the marble floor,
as they formed a circle in front of the
altar, cutting off all retreat for the duke
and his myrmidons.

For once in his life the duke was
abashed. He lost all presence of mind.

The fire in his eye was quenched. He shrank back a craven coward before the glances of my *fiancé*, who stood towering over him like the archangel Michael, with his aureole of bright hair.

"Miserable wretch!" cried Bertie. "If this were not God's house, I would strike you to the ground. Cur! coward! *canaille!*"

"Who are you that speaks to me in this insolent tone?" asked the duke, trying to put a bold face on it. "An English adventurer, by your looks—a meddler in other people's business, like all your nation of prigs and preachers."

"I am minding my own business. I am here to rescue an English lady from the clutches of an Italian blackguard."

"How dare you, sir?" cried the duke, foaming at the mouth with impotent fury. "You shall pay for your insolence to an Italian nobleman. I would challenge you to meet me with your sword, if you were a gentleman; but you are only the bully of an opera-singer. I know your sort well."

"Insult me as much as you like, Duke of Maladetta. Every insult from a creature like you is a compliment to an honest man. But, by God, if you foul with your lips the name of the woman I love and respect, I will drag you out of the chapel and kick you down the steps of this house, as if you were a dog!"

"Enough of this rhodomontade. You seem to think this is the stage of a theatre. What brings you here, and this motley crew of brigands? I am ashamed to see Italian uniforms amongst you. A noble alliance! Italian solders and English cut-throats."

"I arrest you in the name of the King," said the officer in command, coming forward and placing his hand on the duke's shoulder.

"On what charge?"

"For the abduction of the Signora Nella Bardi. Produce the lady."

" Where is the lady you dared to carry off from her mother's house?" cried Bertie.

" Here!" I answered, taking hold of his arm; for I had come down from the gallery as soon as my rescuers appeared on the scene. " Here I am, safe, as I never hoped to be. With you for protector, I can defy this wicked man. I no longer fear his diabolical influence. Take me away; take me to my mother!"

" It was you, false woman," cried the duke, " who put Mariuccia up to this foul trick! This *coup de théâtre* is worthy of an opera-singer. It was you who originated this supposititious marriage. She was not clever enough. I loved you once; I hate you now. Beware of the Black Duke! No man or woman ever escaped his vengeance. I will have my revenge; not even your God can save you from that."

The words of blasphemy had scarcely passed his lips, when he uttered a piercing shriek, and fell with a dull crash upon the pavement.

There was no occasion now for man to arrest the Duke of Maladetta. The Almighty had called him to his account. I had no longer to brave his vengeance. The God whom he despised had saved me.

There was only one who mourned his loss, only one who wished him back. One woman's heart still loved the man who had betrayed her. The bride of a few minutes threw herself upon the body of her bridegroom. She kissed his distorted face, and called him all the dear names by which she had called him in the days when he lured her with false love from her home in the Apennines.

I took her hands in mine and tried to unclasp them from the dead man's neck. I spoke to her lovingly, and implored her to come away with me.

"Leave me with my husband," she cried, "my own husband! I love him as

I have always loved him. I will not be forced away. He had no one to love him, no one in the wide world but me. Stand off," she continued, rising from the ground, and looking proudly round her; "all of you, stand off! I am the Duchess of Maladetta. I can, at all events, command my own servants. I am your mistress, and will be obeyed. Take up the duke and carry him to his room."

"Come with me, Mariuccia," I whispered. "This is no place for you."

"I am his legal wife—his duchess. It is the place of a wife to stay by the husband of her love."

"Not his wife," I continued, "his widow. Come with me, duchess."

"Duchess, you call me! Yes, I am a duchess, an honest woman who can look the world in the face. I can now go to my old father and mother and ask to be forgiven. They won't drive the Duchess of Maladetta from their door. Don't drag

me away from my *sposo*. He loved me
once, just for a little; he loved and left
me, but I was not to be cast off so easily.
I followed him, and became his slave.
But now I am his wife. Ha, ha! to
think that simple Mariuccia is a duchess!
Let me give my husband one last kiss. I
loved you, darling, a pure girl; I loved
you, a lost woman; and I love you now,
your own dear wife. Speak to me—just
say one kind word, *caro mio*. God forgive
you! You had a black heart, *sposo amato!*
—never man had a blacker, but I loved
you all the same. I will never cease to
pray for your poor soul. I can pray now
that I am an honest woman. I am a rich
woman, too, and can well pay the priests.
I will spend all my fortune in masses for
your soul. But you will be a long time in
purgatory—a very long time, poor dear!
Take me away, signorina. I will do
whatever you wish. I owe everything to
you. It was you married me to the duke;

it was you made me a duchess. Where
are my servants? Where is my major-
domo?"

"Here I am, duchess."

"See that everything is arranged as befits
your master's rank. Send for watchers,
send for priests, send for flowers. Let no
expense be spared. Let the last of the
house be buried as befits a Maladetta. I
will be chief mourner—I, his widowed
duchess."

"You shall not go alone, duchess. I,
your friend, will follow your husband to
the grave. I will stand by your side."

"Friend! Do you call yourself the
friend of such as me?"

"A dear friend. You have saved me
from worse than death. You have given
me back to life and love, home and happiness. I am your true friend for ever, if
you will let me, duchess."

"Let you! Such a friendship would be
too great an honour. It might lead me to

better things. I was not always wicked. I was once as good and pure as you. I feel as if I had become a child again—a little child;" and the tears came streaming down from her eyes, making runnels through the paint upon her cheeks.

They were tears of real sorrow and of true repentance. There was joy amongst the angels!

END OF VOL. II.

LONDON: PRINTED BY WILLIAM CLOWES AND SONS, LIMITED, STAMFORD STREET AND CHARING CROSS.

www.ingramcontent.com/pod-product-compliance
Lightning Source LLC
Chambersburg PA
CBHW031036120726
47905CB00007B/2209